Lone Star Ranger

Volume 5

A Ranger to Stand With

James J. Griffin

*For my friend
Ned
Best wishes!*

A Ranger to Stand With by James J. Griffin
Copyright 2015 by James J. Griffin
Cover design by Livia J. Washburn
Texas Ranger badge image courtesy of the Texas
Ranger Hall of Fame and Museum, Waco
Author photo credited to Susanne Onatah
All Rights Reserved

Painted Pony Books
www.paintedponybooks.com
ISBN-13: 978-1511489485
ISBN-10: 1511489480

Lone Star Ranger:

A Ranger to Ride With
A Ranger to Reckon With
A Ranger to Fight With
A Ranger's Christmas
A Ranger to Stand With

For my brother, William,
and his companion, Joanne.

Prologue

Nearly two months had passed since Christmas. It was now the middle of February. Nate Stewart leaned against the adobe wall of the building behind him. His mind drifted back to everything that had happened to him over the past several months. It had certainly been an eventful time in his life.

Nate's father had decided to transplant his family from their comfortable life in Wilmington, Delaware, to a hardscrabble ranch outside San Saba, on the Texas frontier. Unlike his older brother, Jonathan, who had taken to cowboy life easily, the transition had been difficult for Nate. He'd hated the isolated ranch, the small cabin which was their new home, the hot weather, Texas, and everything about it. A band of raiders had attacked the ranch, leaving Nate for dead, and orphaning him. It was only good fortune a patrol of Texas Rangers came across him, treated his hurts, and arranged for him to return home to Delaware.

However, Nate's mind had changed after the attack. He was determined to remain in Texas, and find the men who had murdered his family. That had seemed impossible, until Fate stepped in, and he saved the life of Ranger Jeb Rollins. Jeb decided there was something hidden deep inside the youngster that no one, not even Nate, had realized was there. Call it guts, sand, bravery, courage, or whatever you wished, that one moment convinced Jeb that Nate had what it took to become a Ranger. Of course, since he was only fourteen, Nate was too young—by four years—to become a full-fledged Ranger. So, Jeb planned to arrange with his commanding officer, Captain Dave Quincy, for Nate to be taken on as a camp helper. Instead, Quincy had signed Nate on as a probationary Ranger, skirting the age requirement by listing Nate's birth date as "unknown". Quincy's decision had proved to be the right one when the same band of renegades which had murdered Nate's family attacked the Ranger camp. It was only Nate's alertness which had saved the entire camp from being wiped out.

Since then, Nate had learned not only how to survive, but to thrive, on the harsh Texas frontier. He'd learned how to ride a horse, shoot, fight, and how to keep ever ready for danger. He'd been taught by Percy Leaping Buck, the Rangers' Tonkawa Indian scout, how to track, and how to find food in the often unforgiving Texas wilderness. He'd even nearly been drowned when he fell into rain-swollen Blue Creek and was swept away into the Rio Grande, ending up in Mexico.

Unlike the naïve, scrawny, frightened kid he was when the Rangers found him, he had toughened up. He could stay in the saddle for hours, and go for days on only a few bites of jerky, a couple of swallows of water, and snatches of sleep. He and another young Ranger, Hoot Harrison, had stopped a bank robbery and had helped fight off the same band of outlaws again when they attacked a ranch where Nate and Hoot were visiting. Nate had shot several men, and been shot himself.

Most importantly, as far as he was concerned, he'd

finally killed the leader of the outlaw gang which had murdered his mother, father, and brother, and several of his fellow Rangers. The entire outlaw band had been killed during that final confrontation.

After that gunfight, Captain Quincy offered Nate the opportunity to resign from the Rangers and return home to Delaware. Nate turned him down flat. He'd grown to love Texas, and being a Ranger.

Nate smiled to himself at the thought of how much his life had changed.

1

"Ow!" A bullet smacking into the wall, just alongside Nate's head, sent shards of adobe stinging into his cheek. That bullet brought him back to the present, fast. He leveled his pistol, a big Smith and Wesson .44 American which had belonged to his late brother, as another bullet just missed his ribs. He thumbed back the hammer.

Nate and the small group of Rangers he'd been assigned to had come upon a band of fourteen men attacking an isolated *rancho*, hard on the Mexican border, about twenty miles south of Presidio. Riding heedlessly into the midst of the bunch, the Rangers quickly dispatched six of the men with bullets in their chests. What they hadn't realized until too late was the gang had seven more members, who had remained hidden in a canyon, watching in case anyone did happen to come along and interfere with their plans. They intended to kill all the inhabitants of the *rancho,* loot and burn the place, then run off the livestock, driving it across the Rio Grande into Chihuahua. This group had swept in behind the Rangers, and gotten them pinned down. Now, Joe Duffy was lying stretched out and unmoving in the dusty front yard, blood pooling around his head. Along with the downed Ranger were the bodies nine or ten outlaws, as well as three of the *rancho's vaqueros*. Nate was caught between a horse trough and the stable's wall, while Hoot, Dan, and Jeb had taken cover behind the pillars of the main house's arched veranda. Slowly, the accurate fire of the Rangers, along with that from the house, had taken its toll on the raiders. Four more lay dead, two more had ridden out of the fight, slumped over in their saddles, badly wounded.

Nate took careful aim at the man shooting at him, lining up the barrel of his six-gun on the man's middle. He pulled the trigger, fired, and the man fell back on his butt, with a loud grunt. He sat there, doubled over, one hand pressed to his gut, moaning. Seeing yet another of their number fall, the remaining outlaws turned their horses and galloped away, with Ranger bullets hurrying them along. Nate jumped up from his hiding place. When he did, the man he had just shot raised his pistol and pointed it at Nate's chest. Before he could thumb back the hammer and pull the trigger, Jeb's gun blasted. His bullet tore into the outlaw's chest, slamming him back, dead.

"Reckon that's the last of 'em. We'll catch up with those others that ran later. Dan, you check on Joe," Jeb ordered. "Hoot, help me'n Nate make sure there's no fight left in any of these *hombres*. Nate, let's check on that last one. You forgot to make certain he was finished, kid."

Nate shook his head. "I'm sorry, Jeb. I thought for certain he was done for. I nailed him dead center."

"Let's just see about that," Jeb said. "And you'd be even sorrier if he'd plugged you, just because you got careless." They reached the body of the outlaw. The dead renegade was lying on his back, his eyes staring unblinkingly into the blinding midday sun. A bloody hole, where Jeb's bullet had struck, was just to the left of the center of his chest. His belt buckle was badly dented, stark evidence of where

Nate's bullet had hit.

"See, Jeb. I told you I got him dead center," Nate grumbled.

"Yup, you certainly did," Jeb answered. "And that's the problem. You aimed at his belt buckle, didn't you?"

"Yeah, I did," Nate said. "I'm just doin' what you taught me, to aim at the middle of the target."

"Yup, but you don't aim right *at* a man's belt buckle," Jeb said. "If an hombre's wearin' a thick metal buckle, like this one is, your bullet'll likely knock him down, but it probably won't finish him, or even knock him out of the fight. So, you aim just *above* the buckle. A bullet through the guts there'll sure enough put a man down for keeps." Jeb paused, and grinned a wicked grin. "Of course, if you think the other man's gonna beat you to the shot, and you don't have time to get your gun up high enough, then you plug him just *below* his belt buckle. You can also do that if you're just feelin' particularly ornery, too. Even if your shot doesn't kill that man, he'll wish it had. I reckon you learned a lesson here today, Nate."

"I guess I did," Nate answered, chagrined. "I'd imagine I nearly got myself killed, too. Reckon I have to thank you for savin' my life, Jeb...again."

"*Por nada.* Don't mention it," Jeb answered. "You're still young, and even though you're becomin' a fine Ranger, you've still got a lot to learn. Just remember what happened here today, and you'll be all right."

They turned at a groan behind them. Joe Duffy, with Dan's help, had sat up. Blood trickled from a long bullet slash along his forehead.

"Joe!" Jeb exclaimed. "We thought for certain you were a goner. Looks like you sure fooled all of us. Thank the Lord for that. How bad you hurtin', pardner?"

"It ain't all that bad," Joe answered, trying, but failing, to keep the pain from his voice. "I've had hangovers lots worse'n this. This ain't nothin' but a..." Joe's voice trailed off, and he grimaced.

"Don't try pullin' the wool over my eyes, Joe," Jeb told him.

"All right. I've got one whale of a headache, and I'm bleedin' like a stuck pig," Joe answered. "But my skull's too thick for a bullet to puncture. I'll be fine, after a bit."

"I'm gonna get some bandages and salve from my saddlebags, so I can patch you up," Dan said. "You gonna be okay until I get back?"

"I reckon I can manage," Joe said.

"Good." Dan headed for his horse.

The occupants of the house had come outside, and were helping Hoot check the bodies of the fallen outlaws.

"Any of those *hombres* still alive, Hoot?" Jeb asked.

Hoot shook his head. "Nary a one. The three *vaqueros* are dead, too."

"That's a plumb shame, about the *vaqueros*, that is," Jeb said. "No one'll miss those renegades. They got what they had comin' to 'em. I reckon the ones who got away won't stop runnin' until they hit New Mexico Territory."

The owner of the *rancho* came up to Jeb. He was carrying a rifle, its barrel still warm.

"*Senor*, I am Don Carlos Castellon, the owner of *Rancho Santiago*," he introduced himself. "*Mi familia* and I are most grateful for your help. We couldn't have held off those *banditos* without your assistance."

Like most Texans of Spanish ancestry who lived along the Mexican border, Castellon's speech was a mixture of formal Spanish-accented English and the informal twang of the native Texan.

7

"Sergeant Jeb Rollins. Pleased to meet you, Senor Castellon. We were just doin' our job," Jeb said. "And luckily, we were in the right place at the right time."

"Nevertheless, we are thankful. Don't concern yourselves about getting rid of the bodies of these raiders. We will drag them into the canyon, and leave them for the scavengers. Bring your wounded friend inside, where my wife can care for him properly. And you and your *companeros* will spend the night, of course. Tomorrow, we will bury the bodies of my *vaqueros*. And please, call me Don Carlos."

"As long as you call me Jeb. We don't want to put you out, Don Carlos."

"Nonsense. If you hadn't arrived when you did, those raiders would have destroyed our *rancho*, and no doubt murdered us all. You must be tired, and your wounds should be tended to. I can see the young man with you has also been injured," he said, indicating Nate.

"He's right, Nate. Looks like you've got a pretty good cut on your cheek there," Jeb said. "Reckon you should get that taken care of. Okay, Don Carlos, we'll spend the night. But we'll stay in the bunkhouse. We don't want to be in your way."

During the excitement and fear of the gun battle, Nate hadn't realized the adobe chips which struck his face had dug into his flesh far more deeply than he had thought. He touched his fingers to his right cheek. They came away sticky with blood. His cheek began to burn.

"Excellent," Don Carlos replied to Jeb. "However, as my guests, you will spend tonight in my *hacienda*. Don't argue, Jeb," he continued, when Jeb started to object. He called to one of his *vaqueros*, who hurried over to him.

"Pedro!"

"*Si*, Don Carlos?"

"Our Ranger *amigos* will be spending the night. See to their horses."

"Of course, Don Carlos."

"Pedro, we'll go with you, and get our gear," Jeb said.

"You mind gettin' our stuff for us, Jeb?" Dan asked. "I'd like to get Joe inside. He's bleedin' pretty heavy."

"Sure, you go on ahead," Jeb told him. "We'll be along, quick as we can."

"Follow me, *Senores*," Pedro said. Jeb, Hoot, and Nate got their mounts, along with Joe's and Dan's, then trailed behind Pedro. He led them into a spacious, airy stable, built, as were most structures in this arid land, where wood suitable for building was scarce and expensive, of adobe. Adobe was also favored because its thick walls made structures cooler in the summer and warmer in the winter. The Rangers' horses were led into stalls, untacked, groomed, and fed.

"Sorry, Red," Nate apologized to his horse, when the sorrel nuzzled his hand, looking for a piece of leftover biscuit. "I've got nothin' left to give you. Mebbe come mornin'. You just chow down on your supper, and get some rest."

Red snorted, then buried his muzzle in a manger full of oats and began munching. Like Nate's pistol, rifle stock, and spurs, Big Red had also belonged to his brother, Jonathan. Satisfied their mounts were set for the night, the three Rangers headed back for the house.

The bodies of the outlaws had already been loaded into a wagon, to be hauled away. The three dead vaqueros had been placed on the veranda and covered with blankets. Don Carlos was praying over them. When he saw the Rangers approaching, he murmured a final prayer, then made the Sign of the Cross.

"Julio, Hector, and Miguel were fine *vaqueros*, and good friends," Don Carlos said. "They shall be greatly missed."

"I'm sorry, Don Carlos," Jeb said.

"It would have been much worse if you hadn't arrived when you did. Please, let's go inside so you can take clean up and take some refreshment. Your young friend also still needs his injuries tended to," Don Castellon answered. He opened the door, and motioned the men inside.

"This way, *por favor.*"

Don Carlos led them down a long corridor, to the kitchen at the back of the house. Two women were tying a clean bandage around Joe's head. Another was at the stove, and yet another taking dishes from a dark walnut cupboard.

"How you doin', Joe?" Jeb asked.

"With these pretty *senoritas* fussin' over me? I'm doin' just fine," Joe answered, grinning.

"He will recover quickly, with a bit of rest," one of the women assured Jeb.

"Yeah. He don't need me anymore," Dan said.

"Jeb, allow me to present *mi esposa, Maria,*" Don Carlos said. "The others are *mis hijas, Luz, Estrella, y Inez.*"

"I'm pleased to meet y'all," Jeb said, removing his hat. "I reckon we should introduce ourselves. I'm Jeb Rollins, and these men here are Hoot Harrison and Nate Stewart. You've already met Joe and Dan."

Hoot and Nate nodded to the women. All of them had the dark features typical of their Spanish heritage. And all of them were extremely pretty.

"Nate, please take a seat in that chair," Maria said,

indicating a heavily carved walnut chair next to Joe. "I will wash and dress your injury. Once that is done, Inez will show you to your bedrooms. Estrella will bring soap, water, and towels so you may wash. Supper will be ready in about two hours. I would think you might like to take a *siesta* until then. We will call you once the table is set."

"*Gracias, senora,*" Jeb answered. While Don Carlos might have given the Rangers permission to call him by his first name, Spanish custom and Western propriety dictated that any married woman of Spanish ancestry be called "*senora*", except by family or close acquaintances.

"*De nada,*" Maria answered. Once Nate was seated, she placed a bowl of hot water, soap, and a clean cloth on the table next to him. She used those to wash out the cuts on his cheek.

"You are fortunate, *senor,*" she said. "The cuts, although they bled quite freely, are not very deep. I will not even place any salve over them, until you are ready to leave in the morning. Tonight, leaving them exposed to the air will help them dry out, and hasten the healing process."

"*Gracias, senora,*" Nate said, once she was finished. He stood up, just as three men entered the kitchen. From their bearing and appearance, it was plain they were the Castellon sons.

"*Padre,* the bodies of those *forajidos* have been disposed of," the eldest said.

"Good, good," Don Carlos answered. "Rangers, permit me to introduce *mis hijos, Diego, Benedicto, Juan, y Pablo. Ninos,* Rangers Jeb Rollins, Joe Duffy, Dan Morton, Nate Stewart, and Hoot Harrison."

Greetings were exchanged, hands shaken.

"Now, all of you out of my kitchen," Maria ordered.

"You'd better listen to *mi madre*, Rangers," Benedicto said, with a laugh. "My father may be the *rey* of the *rancho*, but in this *hacienda, mi madre* is the *reina*. And she is an absolute, undisputed monarch."

"All right," Jeb said, laughing in return. "*Senorita* Inez, if you'll show us to our rooms, we'll get out from underfoot."

"Certainly. Right this way," Inez answered.

"After you and your men have washed and rested, Jeb, I'd like you to join me in the parlor for *vino y cigarros, por favor,*" Don Carlos requested.

"Wine and cigars? That's an invitation we can't turn down," Jeb answered. *"Gracias."*

"Excellent!" Don Carlos replied. "Say, in an hour. Wash up, take a short *siesta*, and we will see you then."

"Much obliged, Don Carlos. *Gracias.*"

Inez led the Rangers down a long corridor. She stopped and opened a door on the right.

"*Senor* Nate, *Senor* Hoot, this will be your room," she said. "It is small, but I am certain you will find it quite comfortable. Estrella will be along shortly with soap, water, and towels."

"*Gracias, Senorita,*" Hoot said.

"*De nada,*" Inez said, then continued to the other men, "*Senores*, this way to your rooms."

"Boy howdy, Nate," Hoot said, once they were inside the room, "If this is the 'small' bedroom, I can't imagine what the large one looks like." He pulled off his boots and stretched out on the bed.

"You've sure got that right, pardner," Nate answered, taking stock of their quarters for the night. The bedroom was at least twenty by twenty feet, its ceiling ten feet high, with windows typical of most adobes, high up and narrow.

It was furnished with dark, heavily carved pieces, including the canopied bed Hoot had already occupied. Tapestries covered the walls, and a thick Navajo rug, the floor.

"We might get lost in this bed," Hoot said. "Can't recall ever bein' on a bed this soft, with covers so thick."

A soft knock came at the door.

"*Senores*, may I come in?" Estrella called. "I have your *suministros de bano.*"

"Sure, c'mon in," Nate answered. Hoot jumped off the bed when the door opened, and the young woman entered. She carried three pitchers of hot water in one hand. Over her arm were draped several towels and washcloths.

"*Senor*, you did not have to get up," she said. "I did not mean to make you uncomfortable."

"I...you—I mean, you didn't, *senorita*," Hoot stammered. "It's just that—that well, it wouldn't be proper, that's all, me lyin' in bed with a young lady in the room. It just wouldn't be seemly."

"But we were not alone. Your *amigo* is with you, and the door is open," Estrella answered. "There was nothing improper. But I do appreciate your concern for my honor, *senor*. I will leave your *jabon, agua, y toallas on el lavabo.*"

"Gracias, *senorita*," Hoot answered.

"Yeah, I mean, *si*. Much obliged, ma'am, I mean, *senorita*," Nate added. He was still not completely fluent in, or comfortable with speaking, Spanish. Learning the native language of Mexico, used in so much of Texas, was another of his ongoing lessons.

"*De nada*," Estrella said. "I will see you at *cena*." She left the room, closing the door behind her.

"You want to wash up first, Hoot, or should I?" Nate asked.

"You go first," Hoot said. "I just want to enjoy this fine feather bed awhile longer."

"All right." Nate pulled off his shirt and bandanna, poured water from the pitcher into the basin and ducked his face into it. Then, he took the soap, lathered up one of the washcloths, and began to scrub his face.

"The Castellons sure have some fine-lookin' daughters, don't they, Hoot?" he asked.

"They sure do," Hoot said. "Too bad we won't be stayin' here long enough to get to know 'em better."

"Are they even pretty enough to make you forget Clarissa Hennessey?"

"Did they make you forget Consuela, Nate?"

Nate shook his head. "Not a chance of that."

"Then, they sure didn't make me forget Clarissa, neither, ya idjit."

Nate finished cleaning up, washing his face, neck, hair, and upper torso, then dried off. Once done, he used the damp towels to wipe as much dust as possible from his clothes and boots. He took his place on the bed, while Hoot got up to wash.

"You weren't wrong about this bed, Hoot," he said. "Even the beds we had back home in Delaware weren't anywhere near as soft as these. A feller could drown in these quilts."

"Just don't fall asleep," Hoot warned him. "Don't forget, we've been asked for wine and cigars. It would be an insult to our host not to be there."

"Don't worry about that," Nate answered, stifling a yawn. "I'll be ready when..." His voice trailed off.

"Sure you will, pard," Hoot said, softly. "Reckon I'd better be the one to stay awake."

Nate had already fallen asleep.

14

◆●◆

An hour later, Hoot shook Nate awake.

"C'mon, pard. Time to get goin'," he ordered. "Drinks and smokes are waitin'."

"Huh? Oh,yeah." Nate sat up and swung his legs over the edge of the mattress. "Reckon I must've dozed off."

"Dozed off? You did more'n just 'doze off'," Hoot said, laughing. "You were sawin' logs faster'n a Minnesota lumberjack. Don't believe I've ever heard anyone who can snore as loud as you, Nate. Hurry up, will ya?"

"Be ready in a minute." Nate stamped into his boots, shrugged back into his shirt, and tied his bandanna around his neck.

"I guess I don't need my hat or my gun," he said.

"Well, you don't need your hat, but I'd recommend you strap on your gun," Hoot said. "Those raiders might have had friends, who could be on their way here right now. Or mebbe another band'll show up. I thought we learned you by now the only time a Ranger ever takes off his gun is when he's takin' a bath, or when he's sleepin', and even then, he keeps it close by."

"What about when he's with his girl, and mebbe they're sparkin'?" Nate asked.

"That would depend on the girl, I guess," Hoot answered. "From what I hear tell, around some women you'd want to keep your gun handy. There are women out there as likely to rob, cheat, or kill you as quick as any man. So buckle on your gunbelt and let's go."

"All right."

Nate and Hoot had passed the parlor on their way in, so they knew how to return there without any assistance from one of the Castellons. The parlor was large,

15

furnished, as were all the rooms, with dark, heavily carved furnishings, and decorated with Aztec and Mayan artifacts. Along with Don Carlos and his sons, the other Rangers were already in the room, holding unlit cigars.

"Ah! Hoot and Nate, there you are!" Don Carlos exclaimed. "We've been waiting for you. I was about to send Diego to look for you."

"Nate kinda fell asleep, and I had a devil of a time wakin' him up," Hoot answered.

"Well, at least your *amigo* had not fallen into the final sleep, and actually met *el diablo,*" Don Carlos answered, to general laughter. "It does not matter. You are here now. Please, take a *cigarro* and a glass. The *cigarros* are from Mexico City, and the *vino* pressed from grapes from my own vineyard."

Don Carlos picked up a humidor of cigars from a corner table. He held them out to the two young Rangers. Hoot chose one, then, seeing Nate hesitate, nudged him in the ribs.

"Go ahead, take one," he urged. Nate took a cigar from the humidor.

"Fine. Now, I will pour the drinks," Don Carlos said. He crossed the room to a sideboard, on which stood a silver tray holding three cut crystal decanters full of a deep burgundy colored liquid, and another tray holding cut crystal glasses.

"Nate, I know you don't smoke," Hoot whispered to his friend, "but it would've been downright rude not to take the cigar *Senor* Castellon offered. You don't have to smoke it. Just take one puff on it, then just hold onto it. Besides, you might not have taken to smokin' cigarettes, but cigars may be more to your likin'."

"I doubt it," Nate answered.

Juan and Pablo passed out glasses, which were then filled by Don Carlos. Once everyone had a full glass, he called for attention.

"I would like to propose two toasts," he announced. "First, to the memories of our *companeros,* Hector Mendoza, Miguel Fuentes, and Julio Escobar. They were fine *vaqueros*, and fine *amigos."* He lifted his glass. "To you, Hector, Miguel, and Julio." The other men echoed his sentiment, and took swallows of their wine.

"Now, my second toast is to our Ranger *amigos,* who helped save the *Rancho Santiago* from ruin at the hands of those *banditos,* and who quite possibly saved all of our lives. To the Texas Rangers!"

"To the Texas Rangers!" came the answering shout; then, the glasses were emptied.

"Don Carlos, we are most grateful for your hospitality, and your kind words," Jeb said. "However, we Rangers could not have stopped those renegades by ourselves. It took the help of your brave family, and your brave men, to do that. So, if you would be so kind as to refill our glasses, I would like to propose two toasts of my own."

"Of course, Jeb," Don Carlos said. "I will do that with great pleasure." Everyone's glass was quickly filled, once again.

"First, to the *hombres* of Rancho *Santiago,* the brave *ninos* of the Castellon *familia,* to *Senora* Castellon, and to the beautiful *ninas* of *Senor* and *Senora* Castellon," Jeb proclaimed. His sentiment was answered, with gusto.

"Second, to our gracious host, the *Patron* of *Rancho Santiago,* Don Carlos!" Jeb toasted.

"To Don Carlos!"

"*Muchas gracias,*" Don Carlos said, after the toast was drunk. "You are most kind, you and your men, Jeb. We

17

will be proud to call you *amigos*."

"And us also, for you, your *familia*, and your *hombres*," Jeb answered. "I'd also like to add this is mighty fine *vino*."

"*Gracias*," Don Carlos said. "There is plenty more, so let it flow freely."

Glasses were refilled, cigars lit. Soon, blue smoke filled the air. Nate allowed his cigar to be lit, then, reluctantly, took a puff. He nearly choked, but somehow managed to keep from breaking into a fit of coughing.

"Real smooth, huh?" Hoot asked.

"Yeah. Smooth as a cocklebur stuck between my saddle and my butt," Nate answered. "I'll just hold onto this smelly thing until it burns itself out."

"Just hang onto it until I finish mine, then I'll smoke yours for you," Hoot offered.

"You've got a deal, Hoot."

For the next forty-five minutes, the men smoked, drank, and made conversation. The room fell silent at a knock on the door frame.

"Papa," Luz called. "The *cena* is ready."

"Excellent," Don Carlos said. "Gentlemen, come. Let us eat!"

◆●◆

Jeb and his men were taken into a large dining room, at the center of which was a massive table that seated twenty. A striped cloth covered the entire table, and heavy, multi-colored plates, glasses, cups, and saucers were arranged on that, complemented by heavy silverware. In the center of the table were two heaping platters of roasted lamb. Along with that were bowls of tortillas, squash, chilies, rice, and beans. A sideboard held even more food, along with more wine, and two steaming pots of coffee.

"Gentlemen, allow me to show you your places," Luz told the Rangers. She escorted them to their seats. They remained standing until *Senora* Castellon, Estrella, and Inez joined them.

"*Por favor*, be seated," the *senora* said.

"All right," Jeb answered. "May we help you with anything?"

"No. You are our guests, s*enor,*" Maria said. "Just take your places."

"All right," Jeb agreed. He motioned to his men to sit down.

"We always say Grace before our meals," Don Carlos explained. He folded his hands and bowed his head, as did his family. The Rangers followed their example.

"*Bendicenos, o Dios, y estos dones tus, que estamos a punto de reciber de tu generosidad, por Christo, Nuestro Dios. Amen.*"

"Amen," everyone responded.

"*Ahora, que comemos!*" Don Carlos exclaimed.

Platters of food were passed. Usually, Mexican families, or Texas families of Spanish origin, took their main meals earlier in the day, around noontime, with supper being lighter fare. However, with no one having eaten due to the attack on the *rancho*, and in honor of their new Ranger friends, tonight supper at the *Rancho Santiago* would be the main meal of the day.

The meal consisted of several courses, and lasted almost three hours, concluding with dessert, traditional Mexican flan. After that, the men returned to the parlor for final cigars and more wine, while the women bustled about the dining room and kitchen, cleaning up. It was well past midnight by the time everyone went to bed.

"I don't think I'm gonna be able to move for a week,

Nate," Hoot said, as he undressed.

"Me neither, but you can bet your hat Jeb'll have us on the trail soon as it's light enough to travel," Nate answered.

"Seein' where we're at, this close to old Mexico, that should be 'bet your *sombrero*'," Hoot said. "And we won't be headin' out at sunup. Not this time. Don't forget, we'll be stayin' for the burial of those dead *vaqueros*. And the Castellons aren't gonna let us leave without breakfast. They already told us that. So we get to sleep in, for once."

"And I'm sure lookin' forward to that," Nate said. He finished undressing, then slid under the covers. "G'night, Hoot."

"G'night, Nate."

◆●◆

The next morning, just after sunrise, the three murdered *vaqueros*, Hector Mendoza, Miguel Fuentes, and Julio Escobar, were buried on a hill overlooking the Rio Grande. After prayers were said over them, and the graves filled in, everyone returned to the house for breakfast. Since this was a memorial meal, after the funerals, all of the *Rancho Santiago vaqueros*, the other ranch workers, and their families, were also invited to the meal. Once it was over, Jeb and his men saddled their horses, mounted, and prepared to ride out.

"Rangers, you are welcome back here anytime," Don Carlos said.

"And you at our camp, should you ever come up that way," Jeb answered. "*Adios.*"

"*Vaya con Dios,*" Don Carlos replied.

"Let's go, men," Jeb ordered. He put Dudley into a walk.

♦●♦

"Men," Jeb said, as they rode along. "I want to compliment you on doin' a fine piece of work yesterday. Not just by drivin' off those renegades. That's our job. But we made friends with the Castellons. I don't have to tell you Anglos and Mexes don't get along all that good in Texas. What you did just might help mend some fences, and I appreciate that. Thanks."

"Those folks are a fine family," Dan said. "Goes to show there are good, and bad, on all sides, from all countries, and in all races."

"It's just a doggone shame, in our line of work, we deal mostly with the bad," Joe noted. "But mebbe someday that'll change."

"Mebbe," Jeb answered. "But until then, we'll keep ridin'. And speakin' of dealin' with the bad. Nate, seein' you plug that *hombre* right in his belt buckle reminded me of somethin'. I never taught you the art of the fast draw. You'll recollect I told you that could wait, until your shootin' was accurate."

"You don't need to worry about that, Jeb," Hoot said, laughing. "You saw what Nate's slug did to that belt buckle. He kilt it, good and dead. I reckon we don't have to worry about bein' attacked by any renegade belt buckles as long as ol' Nate's ridin' with us."

"Mebbe so," Jeb answered. "But I've waited too long to teach Nate how to draw, fast and accurate. As soon as we get back to camp, I'm gonna rectify that situation. C'mon, Dudley, get on up there."

He spurred his paint into a lope.

21

2

Since being forced to split his company up into several smaller patrols, Captain Quincy hadn't set any firm schedule for his men to report back to the Circle Dot E. Ranging over hundreds of square miles, searching for outlaws, maintaining any kind of schedule was nearly impossible, anyway. As long as a patrol didn't stay out more than a month, the men returned to the Hennesseys' ranch whenever they had covered an assigned area, one or more of the men had been injured or wounded badly enough to require medical care, or when they needed to resupply.

Four days after leaving the *Rancho Santiago*, Jeb and his men rode back into the Circle Dot E yard. Apparently, another patrol had also just returned, for several of the other Rangers were in the large corral Charlie Hennessey had provided for their horses. They waved when Jeb's patrol approached.

"Howdy, Jeb," Jim Kelly called out. "You're gettin' back right behind us."

Jim's patrol included Carl Swan, Shad Bruneau, and Ken Demarest.

"Seems so," Jeb answered, as he swung out of his saddle. "You boys run into much trouble?"

"Nothin' out of the ordinary," Jim said. "The usual run-ins we have with rustlers. And thankfully, none of the men got hurt." He pulled the saddle off his palomino, Sun Drop. His other mount, Dooley, nuzzled his cheek and whickered impatiently.

"I'll take care of you in a minute, Dooley," Jim told the strawberry roan. A few of the Rangers had two mounts. Jim was one of those. "Gotta see to Sun Drop first. He's been carryin' me for the last thirty miles, so you can just wait." To Jeb he continued, "How about you boys?"

"About the same," Jeb answered. "We did come upon a real bad bunch raidin' a *rancho* a few days' ride from here. Place is called *Rancho Santiago*, owned by a real fine family, name of the Castellons. Between them and us, we took care of the outfit. And, just like you boys, we got lucky. Our only hurts were Joe, who took a bullet across his scalp, and Nate. He got cut by some adobe chips a slug sent into his cheek. But Nate did manage to kill himself a real vicious belt buckle."

"You ain't ever gonna let me live that down, are you, Jeb?" Nate grumbled.

"Not for a while, anyway," Jeb answered.

"Don't let Jeb get you riled up, Nate," Jim advised. "I've killed a belt buckle or two in my time, too. Well, soon as we're done here, I reckon I'd best look up Cap'n Quincy and make out my report. I'll see you at the bunkhouse."

"See you there, Jim."

◆●◆

Once the horses were rubbed down and fed, the men headed for the spare bunkhouse they were using as a headquarters until spring, when the building would be needed for the spring gather and branding hands. Besides the usual main room with its rows of bunks, two long tables and benches for meals, a few card tables and chairs, and a wood-burning stove, this bunkhouse also had a cook shack in an attached lean-to, a small washroom, another room where gear could be stowed, and a small office for the head wrangler, or the ranch's *segundo*. Captain Quincy had taken this for his use. He came out to greet the returning men, then motioned Jim and Jeb into his office. While they made their reports, the others cleaned up, then settled back on their beds.

"Boy howdy, I sure hope we get to stay here for a couple of days, at least," Nate said. He was picking up more of the cowboy's lingo every day. "My saddle sores have saddle sores."

"It might happen, but I wouldn't count on it," Hoot said. "As long as I've been ridin' for the Rangers, it seems like as soon as we might get a few days off, some new trouble pops up somewhere, and we're on the way again."

George Bayfield, the company cook, stuck his head in from the cook shack.

"Supper'll be ready in about an hour, boys," he said.

"That sounds good," Carl called from his bunk. "I missed too many meals this last time out."

"Swan, I ain't been with the Rangers but a couple of months," Shad said, laughing. "However, one thing I have learned is you ain't never missed a chance to chow down."

"He's got you pegged, Carl," Ken added.

"Quit ridin' Carl," George said. "At least he always appreciates my cookin'. He's not forever complainin' about it like most of you. Carl, I'll save you an extra piece of pie."

"Thanks, George. I'm grateful," Carl said.

George ducked back inside the cook shack. The other men relaxed for the next hour, some dozing off, others mending shirts or darning socks, one or two cleaning their guns, the rest talking about their latest experiences on the trail. When George asked for help bringing out the steaks, boiled potatoes, and black-eyed peas that would be supper, he had no shortage of volunteers. After days or weeks on the trail, eating mostly bacon, beans, and hardtack, a full meal would be a welcome change.

The men made short work of their suppers. They were working on their pie and coffee, along with cigarettes for many of them, when Captain Quincy banged a spoon against his coffee cup for attention. The room immediately fell silent.

"Men," he announced. "I've taken a quick look at Jim and Jeb's reports. It appears you've done fine jobs, and I thank you all."

"No need to thank us, Cap'n," Ken said. "It's all part of the territory."

"Nonetheless, I'm grateful," Quincy answered. "Now, there are still several other patrols out there, as you know. You men have worked hard the past few weeks. I have no specific reports of trouble at this time, so I'm going to allow y'all a week's rest. That will be rescinded, of course, if any trouble does flare up."

"Rescinded? What's that mean?" Hoot whispered to Nate.

"It means cancelled, or, in other words, we can *forget* that rest," Nate answered.

"Oh."

"However, this time of year, with the weather so uncertain, outlaw activity does tend to die down, so I don't expect to have to cut your time short," Quincy continued. "If any of you feel you'd like to ride into Presidio and do some celebratin', that's fine, as long as you're back here in a week. Personally, I'd recommend you just stay here at the Hennesseys' and rest up."

Quincy was answered with a chorus of thanks.

"You want to head up to Presidio, Nate?" Hoot asked. "See if we can rustle us up some fun?"

"Nah. I'd just like to hang around here, mebbe get to know Consuela a bit better," Nate answered. "Unless you really want to ride to town."

"Not especially," Hoot said. "I've seen enough of the back of my horse's ears for now. I'm with you. We'll just stay right here, and visit with our gals."

Jeb wandered over and sat next to them.

"Nate, since we're not gonna be doin' anythin' for the next few days, this'll be the time for you to learn the fast draw. Right after breakfast tomorrow suit you?"

"That'll suit me just fine," Nate agreed.

"Good. Hoot, I'd like you to come along too," Jeb said.

"I was already plannin' on it," Hoot answered. "You don't think I'm gonna miss this, do you?

Jeb chuckled. "I should've figured as much. Now, I'm gonna get me some shut-eye. See you in the mornin'.'"

"See you, Jeb."

◆●◆

The next morning, after having their breakfast, Jeb, Nate, and Hoot gathered their six-guns, Jeb a box of cartridges, and walked toward an arroyo that cut across one corner of the Circle Dot E, not far from the buildings.

"What'cha up to?" Josiah Hennessey called after them.

Josiah was the youngest of the Hennessey children. He was only seven, while his older siblings were all in their teens—Luke, his nearest brother in age, being sixteen. Since the Rangers had arrived at the Hennessey ranch, Josiah had developed a serious case of hero worship for the rugged lawmen.

"We're headin' over to the arroyo, to teach Nate the fast draw," Jeb answered.

"Can I come along and watch?" Josiah pleaded. "I ain't got nothin' to do. My brothers are out lookin' for strays, my pa's busy in his office, and my sisters ain't no fun."

"Sure," Jeb agreed. "C'mon."

"Oh, boy. Just let me get my gun."

"Well, you'd better hurry," Jeb told him.

"I'll be back in a jiffy," Josiah promised. He ran back to the house and returned a moment later with an old Colt stuck behind his belt. The firing pin had long since been worn off, but as far as Josiah was concerned, he'd killed an awful lot of outlaws and renegade Indians with that old gun.

"I'm ready, Ranger Jeb," he said.

"Then, let's go," Jeb answered. "We're burnin' daylight."

With Josiah tagging along, they reached the arroyo a few minutes later.

"Josiah, you sit on that rock, where you can watch, but won't be underfoot," Jeb ordered the boy.

"Sure, Ranger Jeb." Josiah scurried over to the rock and plopped himself down. "This all right?"

"That's fine," Jeb assured him. He turned to Nate. "Nate, I've got somethin' else I want to teach you, before we start your fast draw lessons," he told him.

"I'm ready for whatever you want to throw at me," Nate answered.

"We'll see," Jeb answered. "First, both you and Hoot, empty your pistols. Make certain there's no live bullets left in the chambers."

"All right," Nate said. Hoot was already punching the bullets out of his gun. Jeb also emptied his six-gun. He opened the box of cartridges he'd brought, took out a handful, and passed the box to Hoot.

"Take a bunch of those and stuff 'em in your pocket, then load your gun. Nate, you do likewise."

"Sure," Hoot said, with a grin. He'd had this same lesson from Jeb when he'd joined the Rangers, and knew what was coming. He took a handful of cartridges from the box, then passed it to Nate, who did the same.

"Guns all loaded?" Jeb asked, a moment later.

"Yep," Hoot said.

"Mine too," Nate added.

"Good. Now, Nate, these bullets we'll be usin' today are blanks. And we *will* be drawin' and shootin' at each other. That's the best way to learn. But, just because they're blanks, that doesn't mean they're not dangerous. A blank cartridge still holds a full charge of powder. The only difference is, instead of a lead slug, it's got a wad of paper or cardboard. But there's still enough power behind it to put a hole through a tin can at ten feet. When we're practicin', you're gonna feel it when you get hit by one of these slugs. Okay?"

"I reckon," Nate said. "Can't be any rougher than learnin' how to knife fight from Hoot."

"You're about to find out, pard," Hoot said.

"Enough jabberin'," Jeb said. "Nate, time for your first lesson. I want you to stand, facin' me, about six feet back."

Nate backed away six feet. "This all right?"

"That's fine. Now, for this lesson, you're the Ranger. I'm an outlaw you've just caught. Pull out your gun and cover me."

"Okay." Nate lifted his gun from its holster and pointed it at Jeb's chest.

28

"Good. Now, order me to hand you my gun, butt first."

"Sure. Listen, Mister, take out your gun, slow and easy, and hand it to me, butt first," Nate ordered. "No false moves, or I'll drop you right where you stand."

"Okay. Okay, Ranger. You've got me, all right. I'll go peaceable like. Just don't shoot me," Jeb pleaded. He took the gun from his holster, then held it out to Nate, butt first. When Nate reached for it, Jeb, whose trigger finger, unnoticed by Nate, was in the trigger guard, spun the gun level, thumbed back the hammer, and pulled the trigger. A wad of cardboard slammed into Nate's stomach, with enough impact to drive him backward and double him over. Gasping for breath, Nate fell to the dirt.

"And you just got yourself plugged in the gut and killed, Nate," Jeb said. "That's called the road agent's spin. No one knows for certain who first came up with it, but it's cost many a lawman his life. You never, ever ask a man to hand you his gun butt first. It's a sure way to get killed. Either tell him to unbuckle his gunbelt and drop it, or take his gun out of the holster with two fingers, then drop it. Unless, like what just happened, you want a bullet in your stomach. Lesson learned?"

"Lesson learned," Nate said. "I don't reckon I'll ever forget it, neither."

"That was the idea, kid," Jeb answered. He grabbed Nate's hand and pulled him to his feet. "You ready to learn the fast draw now?"

"I sure am," Nate said.

"Good. The first thing to remember is, just like you never ask a man for his gun butt first, you never go after a renegade with your gun still in its holster. You pull out that gun, then you go after him, so you'll most times have him covered before he can try to plug you. If Cap'n Dave,

Lieutenant Bob, me, or any of the other men ever see you goin' after an *hombre* with your gun still in its holster, you'll be finished as a Ranger. *Comprende?"*

"Comprende," Nate said.

"Okay. Now, that said, gunfights do happen, although not nearly as often as they appear in the dime novels," Jeb said. "Another thing to remember, which you already know, is that six-guns ain't all that accurate beyond thirty or forty feet, so, if you can't avoid a showdown, you want to make certain you're close enough to hit your opponent."

"But that means he's also close enough to hit me," Nate objected.

"That's true enough," Jeb conceded. "However, if you take the first shot from too far away and miss, it's most likely the man facin' you will put a bullet in you before you get the chance to pull the trigger again. So, it's best to make sure you're in range, or at least close enough to be fairly certain of your shot. And I shouldn't have to remind you of this, but I'm goin' to. You don't aim for the head, or the legs, or the arms, when someone is shootin' at you. You go for the biggest target, the chest or belly. And if there's any chance that man can still use his gun after you've shot him, you shoot him again. Don't, and you could both be dead...or him pull through, while you'll be six feet under. You always make certain he's dead, or out of the fight."

"You don't have to worry about that, with Ranger Belt Buckle Killer there," Hoot said, laughing.

"Not now, Hoot," Jeb scolded. "This isn't the time for foolin' around. Nate, time for you and me to face each other over loaded guns. You ready? If you are, we'll separate by about twenty feet."

"I reckon," Nate said. Despite the fact he had been in

several gun battles, and had killed the man who had led the gang responsible for the murders of his family, the only other time he'd ever faced a man over a gun was during a bank robbery in San Saba. Despite the fact no gunplay had taken place, once the holdup men were safely behind bars, Nate had gotten so frightened he'd had to rush to the outhouse, on the double. Even now, after months with the Rangers, he still had self-doubts about his ability to handle himself in a one-on-one gunfight. As he walked slowly away from Jeb, sweat popped out on his brow, and his palms grew damp with perspiration.

"That's good," Jeb called, when they were about twenty feet apart. "Now, your holster is right about where you want it, just a tad below your waist. You want to crouch, just a bit, your feet spread slightly. Some men like to turn a bit sideways, to make themselves less of a target. I don't, because it seems to me it's a bit slower draw, standin' that way, plus it just feels like it takes a split second longer to line up your target. Now, get yourself set. When you think you're ready, you hold your hand just over the butt of your gun. Let me know when you're set."

Nate put himself into a crouch, his feet spread. He placed his hand just above his Smith and Wesson's butt.

"I'm ready," he called.

"All right. Three things to remember, all equally important," Jeb answered. "First, always take the fraction of a second you need to make certain of your shot. A lotta times, it's not the man who pulls the trigger first who wins a gunfight, it's the one who takes the time to make certain of his shot.

"Second, never fan the hammer. That's the fastest way to get yourself killed, by sprayin' bullets all over the place while the man you're facin' takes careful aim and plugs you plumb center.

"And third, it's usually hard to figure out exactly when a man's gonna go for his gun. Some men will flex their fingers, others might twitch, some will smile; others, you can see it in their eyes. But mostly you can't tell, at all. Keep that in mind. Now, for the first couple of lessons, I'm gonna make things a bit easier on you. I'll count to three, then we'll go for our guns. And if you get hit, go down. I'll do the same if you get me. I try to make these lessons as real as possible. All right?"

"All right."

"Good. One. Two. Three."

Both men grabbed for their guns. Nate felt his lift smoothly from his holster. He had it almost level when Jeb's shot hit him in the left breast. He grabbed his chest, and spun to the ground.

"You got him, Ranger Jeb!" Josiah shouted, excitedly.

"You all right, Nate?" Jeb called.

"Yeah, yeah, I'm fine," Nate answered, pushing himself to his feet.

"Good. And for your first try, you didn't do half-bad," Jeb encouraged him. "You almost beat me. Let's go again."

"I'm ready for you this time, Ranger," Nate said, with a wicked grin.

"Okay. One. Two. Three."

Again, both men grabbed for their guns. Again, Nate felt the impact of a slug hitting his chest. But this time, as he went down, he saw Jeb grab his belly, and jackknife to the ground.

"Appears to me you both done kilt each other," Hoot called. "I reckon he got you, Jeb."

"He did, Ranger Jeb," Josiah added. "I saw it. He got you right in the guts. You're dead."

"I reckon he did," Jeb answered, as he rolled onto his back, then sat up. He rubbed the sore spot on his belly where Nate's slug had hit.

"Let's go again, Nate. The only way to develop a consistent fast draw is to practice."

"All right, Jeb."

For the next thirty minutes, Jeb and Nate blazed away at each other. While Jeb won most of the fights, Nate beat him to the draw several times.

"You don't have to worry about your draw, Nate," Jeb told him. "You're faster'n a lot of men, and more accurate than most. However, we're not done yet. I want you and Hoot to face each other. That'll give you a feel for how another man might act in a showdown."

"All right," Nate said.

Hoot jumped to his feet.

"I've been lookin' forward to this all mornin'," he said. "Ain't no man alive who can take me over leveled six-guns."

"You've been readin' too many dime novels, Hoot," Jeb said.

"Mebbe so, but I'm still gonna outdraw and gun down that there Nate hombre," Hoot retorted.

"We'll see about that," Nate shot back. He pulled out his gun, then shot Hoot in the ribs. Hoot grabbed his side, hollering.

"You weren't supposed to draw until we were both ready, ya idjit!"

"Just takin' Jeb's lesson to heart," Nate answered, as he slid his gun back in its holster. "Always come after a renegade with gun drawn. And shoot him before he has the chance to shoot you."

"We'll just see about that," Hoot snapped. "Go for your

33

gun."

He grabbed his own pistol, and shot Nate three times, just above his belt.

"Now, who's faster?" he shouted, as Nate fell.

"That don't prove a thing," Nate said. "Except you're a no-good gut-shooter."

"Yeah, but I'm still standin', and you ain't," Hoot retorted.

"If you two are through clownin' around, I'd like to get back to Nate's lesson," Jeb said. "Nate, get back up."

"All right," Hoot said. "I'm ready."

"So am I," Nate added, as he regained his feet.

"Good. Then both of you get out there and get to work," Jeb ordered. "We're not quittin' until all of these blanks are gone."

◆●◆

As Jeb had ordered, Nate and Hoot drew on each other until all of the blank ammunition was used up. They proved evenly matched, with Hoot having a slight edge.

"Nate," Jeb said, once they were finished. "You'll more than do. I know you said your brother was a natural with a six-gun. You ain't, but you've got a smooth draw, a careful aim, and you keep your wits about you. A level head is the most important thing of all. All you need now is more practice. Get that every chance you can."

"Sure. Sure, Jeb," Nate answered. This lesson had proved invaluable to him in a way Jeb would never know. All the nerves he'd had, when the lesson started, about facing a man over leveled pistols, were gone. He now felt confident when he pulled his gun that he would no longer have sweaty palms and jangled nerves. He might get outdrawn and gunned down, but at least he'd have an equal chance.

Jeb looked up at the sun.

"It's gettin' on close to noon," he said. "About time for dinner. Josiah, you want to eat with us?"

"I sure do, Ranger Jeb, but there's somethin' I've gotta do first," Josiah answered.

"And what might that be?" Jeb asked.

"I'm gonna take care of all of ya. Ain't none of ya *hombres* as fast on the draw as me," Josiah said. "I can plug all three of ya before ya even get your guns out of your holsters."

Jeb glanced at Nate and Hoot.

"Oh, ya think so, do ya? We'll just see about that, Josiah. Get ready to go for your gun," he challenged.

"All right, Ranger."

Josiah pulled the old Colt from behind his belt. He thumbed back the hammer, aimed at the Rangers, and pulled the trigger, three times. Jeb clawed at his belly, grunted, doubled over, and pitched to the dirt. Nate and Hoot clutched their chests, yelled in pain, and fell alongside him.

"Told ya I was the fastest gun in Texas," Josiah sneered, standing over the downed Rangers. "Drilled all three of ya, dead center."

"You're...you're the fastest, all right, kid," Jeb gasped. He shuddered and lay still, then looked up at Josiah and grinned.

"I'll bet you're the hungriest, too. Let's go see what George has cooked up."

"All right. Now you're talkin', Ranger Jeb. Let's go."

3

Two days after Nate's quick draw lessons, the wind picked up out of the northwest. The temperature began to drop rapidly, and thick, puffy clouds scudded across the sky. Several of the Rangers, including Jeb, Nate, and Hoot, were grooming their horses when two men rode up.

"Howdy," one of them said.

"Howdy yourselves," Jeb answered. "I'm kinda surprised to see riders out in weather like this. It looks like a blue norther's about to blow in."

"There sure is one brewin'. A big one," the other rider answered. "We just came over the pass. About fifteen miles back, it's already startin' to snow. My handle's Curly, by the way. Curly Thomas. My pard's Deke Vance."

"Jeb Rollins, Hoot Harrison, Nate Stewart, Dan Morton, and Shad Bruneau," Jeb answered. "Pleased to meet you fellers. Anythin' in particular we can help you with?"

"Glad to meet you, also," Thomas said. "We were hopin' mebbe we could hire on here. If not, at least mebbe the owners'll let us stay here until the storm passes. One of you the foreman?"

Jeb shook his head. "Nope. We're Texas Rangers, usin' this ranch for our headquarters. The Hennesseys own the place. You might want to stop at the big bunkhouse, first. Mark Swick's the foreman. I'd imagine he does the hirin'.

Like you mentioned, at the very least you could ask him for a place to hunker down until this storm blows itself out."

On most large ranches, the hiring and firing was done by the ranch foreman, not the owner.

"Much obliged," Thomas said. "C'mon, Deke, let's go."

They turned their horses and headed for the bunkhouse.

"You reckon those two are only chuckline ridin' cowboys, like they claim, Jeb?" Shad asked.

Jeb scratched his jaw before replying.

"I dunno. It's kind of a funny time of year to be lookin' for ranch work. Most spreads aren't hirin' now. The spring gather won't start for another month, at least."

"What's a chuckline ridin' cowboy, Jeb?" Nate asked. "And what the heck is a spring gather?"

"I keep forgettin' there's still a lot about the West you don't know, Nate," Jeb answered. "A chuckline, or grubline, ridin' cowboy is a man who drifts from ranch to ranch, workin' at one for a spell, then movin' on. He doesn't stay in one place for very long. But, most of 'em'll settle at a ranch before winter sets in, and stay there until the weather warms up. That's why it's sorta strange that pair is lookin' for work right now."

"Yeah, it is," Dan agreed, "but they didn't flinch when you told 'em we were Rangers. If they're bent on trouble, they should have shown some sign when they found out who we are."

"That's true," Jeb conceded. "Mebbe they are just drifters, like they claim, and didn't find a place to settle down for the winter. We'll just have to wait and see. But we'd best keep an eye on 'em."

"Jeb, I'd still like to know what a spring gather is," Nate

reminded him.

"Oh, yeah. That's when the mamas and their newborn calves are rounded up, branded, and earmarked."

"Earmarked?" Nate echoed.

"Yeah. Just like every ranch has its own brand, most also earmark their cows. That means they cut, or bob, a piece out of the ear. Each ranch cuts a different way, so the cow is earmarked. Helps to identify 'em, just like the brand," Jeb explained.

"Now, along with the gather, actually part of it most times, there's usually a roundup. That's gettin' together all the steers that are ready for market, along with the cows that are no longer producin' babies, and makin' up a shippin' herd to drive north to the railheads. Most spreads do that in the spring. Then, there are some which wait until later in the summer to put together their shippin' herds.

"A lot of folks use *gather* and *roundup* to mean the same thing. They're not one hundred percent right, but it's not much different. And, as if you ain't confused enough, some ranches even have a fall roundup. And if there's a drought, all bets are off. If a man can't keep his herds fed and watered, he's better off tryin' to get as many of his cows to market as he can, rather'n just watchin' 'em die of thirst or starvation right in front of him."

"Well, lookin' at that sky, I'd say a drought is the least of our worries right now," Shad said. "Dunno about you boys, but I'm gonna finish carin' for my horse, then I'm headin' for the bunkhouse, and a spot next to the stove."

"And I'm gonna 'gather' me some hot coffee," Hoot added.

The sky had thickened and lowered to a dark gray. Already, the first snowflakes were beginning to fall.

"I'd say that's good advice," Jeb agreed. "Let's get these horses settled, then get inside. This is gonna be one heckuva storm."

◆●◆

While large snowstorms were rare in this part of Texas, they did occur, and the one which had just descended on the Hennessey ranch was proving to be a big one. The storm rapidly grew in intensity, and raged all night. The wind howled and moaned through the bunkhouse's eaves. At times, it sounded exactly like a woman's screams. The men huddled around the pot-bellied stove, which glowed red from the fire inside, or crawled into their bunks, adding extra blankets.

"Sure am glad I gave you boys those days off," Captain Quincy said. "I'd hate to have you out in this norther. I hope the rest of the men are hunkered down somewhere."

"This storm? This storm ain't nothin', Cap'n Dave," Nate said.

"I suppose you're gonna tell us the storms in Delaware are a lot worse," Hoot said.

"They sure are. Much worse. This here 'blue norther', as you fellers call it down here, wouldn't be nothin' but a gentle breeze and a few snowflakes back home. We call 'em nor'easters up there."

"And you claim this storm ain't nothin'?" Jeb challenged.

"Nothin' at all," Nate answered. "Why, I recall one storm where it got so cold the Delaware River froze solid, so folks were able to walk clean across to New Jersey. Stayed that way all winter. The snow came down so thick and fast it was clean up to the second story windows in an hour. Folks had to climb up on their roofs and slide off just to get out. People who lived in one floor houses had to dig shafts up through the snow, just like they was tunnelin' a mine. To get around, we had to tunnel through the snow like gophers. When things finally thawed out in the spring, there was at least half a dozen sailin' ships sittin' right smack in the middle of downtown Wilmington. No one could figure out how to get those out of there. We got lucky, though. The snow melted so fast those ships just rode the water right back to the river and out to sea."

"What about the buildin's?" Carl asked. "Didn't they get washed away, too?"

"And didn't a lot of folks drown?" Ken added.

"Nope. Not at all. That storm was a little bigger than most, but it happens every year. Folks just open their doors and use the water for spring cleanin'. And it provides everyone free baths."

"I suppose next you're gonna tell us another whale like the one you claimed done ate up your friend was found in the middle of town, too, Nate," Captain Quincy said, laughing.

"No, the whales are smarter than that," Nate said. "They just wait at the mouth of the river, and swallow up the ships as they get washed by."

"Y'know, Cap'n Dave, somethin's gettin' pretty deep in here, all right, and it sure ain't the snow," Joe said.

"You've certainly got that correct," Captain Quincy answered. He picked up the poker, opened the stove door, and stirred up the fire.

"Cap'n, speakin' of poker, anyone want to play a few hands?" Nate asked.

"Another joke like that and I'll bend this poker over your head," Quincy answered. "But I wouldn't mind a game or two. Anyone else?

"I'm in," Shad said.

"Me, too," Ken added.

"No one else?" Quincy asked. He was met with a shaking of heads.

"Reckon we'll all just try'n stay warm and watch you boys play," Jeb said.

"All right." Quincy, Nate, Shad, and Ken gathered around one of the card tables. While the storm raged around them, they played until the wee hours of the morning.

◆●◆

Sometime before dawn, the storm blew its way into Mexico. It left behind a foot of snow—drifted four feet deep in spots—sunny, cold weather, and a dazzlingly blue sky. Nate looked out the window and jumped from his bunk.

"Hey, Hoot," he called. "It's stopped snowin'. Let's grab our horses and go for a ride."

"Are you plumb loco, Nate?" Hoot answered, burrowing more deeply under his blankets. "It's cold out there."

"C'mon, pard," Nate urged, "It'll be fun. We can bundle up warm enough." He yanked the covers off Hoot. "Let's go."

"All right. All right, ya idjit. But if I freeze to death, I'm gonna come back to haunt you," Hoot answered. He swung his legs over the edge of the mattress and stood up, shivering.

"You ain't ever gonna come back to haunt me, Hoot," Nate retorted. "Not as scared of haints as you are."

"I'll make an exception in your case. Boy howdy, it's even cold inside this doggone bunkhouse," Hoot complained. "And the floor's freezin' on my bare feet."

"That's cause you're not movin'," Nate answered. "And

that cold floor's why I sleep with my socks on. Once we get outside and get movin', you'll warm up right quick. Hurry up."

"Keep it down you two, will ya?" Jim muttered. "The rest of us are still tryin' to sleep."

"We'll be gone in a minute," Nate answered.

Both boys hurriedly dressed, putting on two pairs of socks before stamping into their boots, shrugging into their thick sheepskin coats, shoving gloves into their pockets, then wrapping scarves around their necks and jamming their hats on their heads. When they got to the corral, they whistled up their horses. Nate's sorrel, Big Red, and Hoot's lineback dun, Sandy, trotted up to the fence, snorting and blowing. Steam emitted from their nostrils, and ice coated their whiskers. Snow clung to their fetlocks.

"You ready to go for a run, Red?" Nate asked his horse, as he gave him a piece of leftover biscuit. Red whinnied a reply.

Sandy was pawing at the snow.

"Seems like you're eager to go, too, pal," Hoot said to him. "Just gimme a minute."

"We won't need our saddles, Hoot," Nate said. "Just our bridles. Even if we fall off, we won't get hurt, landin' in the snow."

"You ever rode bareback before, Nate?" Hoot asked.

"Well, no, I haven't," Nate admitted. "But I reckon it's high time I learned."

They got their bridles from the stable, slid the headstalls over their horse's heads and slipped the bits into their mouths, then led them out of the corral. The mounts pranced in their eagerness to run. Nate and Hoot swung onto their backs. Before they could even settle in place, the horses took off at a gallop.

"Hang on, Nate!" Hoot hollered, as he leaned low over Sandy's neck. "Grab Red's mane if you have to, and wrap your legs around his barrel tight as you can. He's probably gonna buck."

He had no sooner said this when Red kicked out his hind legs and lifted his rump in a huge buck. Nate's butt rose a foot off Red's back, then slammed back down. When his crotch hit Red's withers, he yelped in pain. Red then reared, his withers now catching Nate in the belly. Nate grunted, but managed to hang on as Red lined out in a run once again.

Big Red and Sandy raced through the foot deep, powdery snow, seeming to float on air, kicking up plumes of white from their hooves. Red and Sandy were both young animals, rested and full of spirit, as excited by the snow as their riders. They ran for over a mile before slowing to a lope.

"Told ya this'd be fun, Hoot!" Nate shouted. "Just like sittin' in a rockin' chair. Man, it doesn't get any better'n this."

"It sure don't," Hoot answered. "I've gotta admit, you were sure right, Nate. Let's go, Sandy!"

He kicked his dun into a gallop once again.

"Get up there, Red," Nate hollered, letting his sorrel stretch out to catch, then overtake, Hoot's horse.

A mile later, the horses had burned off most of their excess energy. They slowed to a walk. Nate rolled off Red's back, landing in the snow with a thud. Hoot turned Dudley back to where Nate lay on his back, drawing in great draughts of air.

"You all right, Nate?" he asked.

"Sure am, pardner. C'mon down and join me!"

Nate grabbed Hoot's ankle, and pulled him off his horse. Hoot landed on top of him.

"Why you son of a—" Hoot yelled. "I'll take care of you, Nate."

"Just get offa me, you big ape," Nate retorted. He tried to shove Hoot off, but Hoot wrapped his arms around Nate and flipped him over. They were at the edge of a short hill, and Hoot's move sent them rolling over the rim, arms and legs flailing, as they picked up momentum, rolling over and over, faster and faster, until they reached the bottom of the slope, covered with snow. Hoot rolled off Nate, and they lay there, side by side, laughing and gasping for breath.

"Well, was I right?" Nate asked. "Didn't I tell you we'd have a good time, Hoot?"

"Yeah, I reckon you did," Hoot answered. He glanced at the slope. "Except now we've gotta climb back up this hill."

"Well, if you hadn't rolled us over the edge, we wouldn't have to," Nate said.

"Yeah, and if you hadn't pulled me off my horse, we wouldn't be here in the first place," Hoot replied.

"I reckon that's so," Nate admitted. "Well, we won't get back up this hill just lyin' here." He sat up, then pushed himself to his feet.

"Let's hope our horses haven't run off," Hoot said, as he too stood up. "We might as well get at it."

He and Nate began trudging back up the hill.

"Hoot, you ever seen snow before?" Nate asked.

"A little, but never this much, not even when I was a kid up in Arkansas," Hoot answered. "Never more'n an inch or so, and it usually melted right away. Snow ain't all that common in Texas, except mebbe on some of the higher mountains. And we ain't even got a whole lot of those."

"We don't have many in Delaware, either," Nate answered. "In fact, none. You've got to head up into Pennsylvania to find the closest mountains. But we do get a lot of snow. Now, let's save our breath until we get up this hill."

They maintained a steady pace as they climbed, occasionally slipping on an icy patch hidden under the fresh powder. By the time they reached the top, ten minutes later, both were short of breath. To their relief, both horses were close to where they'd left them. They had pawed through the snow, and were tugging at some winter-killed bunch grass.

Nate fell slightly behind Hoot. He reached down and scooped up a handful of snow.

"Hoot," he called.

"What, Nate?" Hoot turned to look back at his partner. When he did, Nate hit him squarely in the face with a huge snowball.

"Got ya, Hoot! Snowball fight!" Nate shouted.

"You think so? Well, I'll just show you, pardner," Hoot retorted. He grabbed some snow, packed it tightly, and let it fly. It knocked Nate's hat off.

"You missed!" Nate yelled, as he sent a return snowball at Hoot. This one bounced off Hoot's shoulder.

"Not this time!" Hoot yelled back. His next snowball took Nate in the middle of his chest, a following one smacking into Nate's belly.

"You give up, Nate?" he asked.

"This ain't over. Not by a long shot," Nate answered. He threw another snowball, this one catching Hoot in the throat. Snow dropped behind Hoot's shirt, soaking his chest. When Nate turned to scoop up more snow, Hoot's

45

next shot caught Nate on the back of his neck. A huge chunk of snow rolled down Nate's back.

For twenty minutes they battled, neither giving in until both were completely plastered with snow and soaked to the skin.

"I reckon I've had enough, Nate," Hoot said, gasping.

"Same here," Nate admitted. He was hunched over, dragging air into his lungs. "I guess we'd better head on back, before Cap'n Quincy or Jeb start wonderin' where we've gotten to."

"Just gimme a minute, first," Hoot said. "I've got a chill from bein' soaked to the skin. I need to pee, real bad."

"So do I," Nate said. He unbuttoned his denims to relieve himself.

"Hey, Nate, bet I can pee farther than you can," Hoot challenged. "It'll be easy to tell in this snow."

"So what? That's not a big deal," Nate answered. "Watch this."

Nate proceeded to write his name in the snow. When he finished crossing the "t", he grinned.

"Think you can do that, Hoot?"

"I reckon I can." Hoot also marked the snow with his name.

"There, Nate. How's that?"

"The 't's' not crossed straight, and you didn't quite finish," Nate answered.

"What d'ya mean, I didn't 'quite finish' You sayin' you want me to write my last name, too? I don't hold that much water, Nate," Hoot protested.

"That's not what I meant," Nate answered. "Watch."

Nate put two dots in the center of the "o's" in Hoot, then spelled out "Owl" underneath that.

"See. Hoot Owl. *Now* your name's finished, pard."

"All right, I reckon you've got me beat," Hoot conceded. "It's just a doggone shame you can't hit a target with your rifle as good."

He laughed, then shivered.

"I'm really startin' to get cold, Nate. We'd best get movin'. That warm stove in the bunkhouse and a hot cup of coffee are sure gonna feel good."

"I'm gettin' a chill too," Nate said. "Let's get on back."

They got their horses, mounted, turned them toward the Circle Dot E, and put them into a trot.

◆●◆

By the time they got back to the ranch, both boys were thoroughly chilled. They took the bridles off their horses and turned them into the corral, making certain they had hay and water, checking their hooves for any ice balls which might have built up inside their shoes, which could easily cause a horse to strain a tendon or even break a leg, then hurried inside the Rangers' quarters. Their teeth were chattering, they were shivering, and their skin had taken on a deathly pale pallor.

"Hoot! Nate! Where in the blue blazes have you two been?" Captain Quincy shouted, when they came through the door. "We were worried you'd gotten lost, or mebbe ran into some renegades or Indians. We were just about ready to start searchin' for you."

"And what the devil have you been up to?" Jeb asked. "You both look half-frozen."

"Nate was showing me how they have fun in the winter, up North," Hoot answered.

"I'm sorry, Cap'n Dave," Nate said. "It's my fault. I saw all that snow out there, and it reminded me of home. I just had to get Big Red and go for a ride. Then Hoot and I got

47

into a wrestlin' match, then a snowball fight, and—"

"Don't say it," Jeb warned him. "You were about to say things *snowballed* from there."

"Well, not exactly, but now that you mention it," Nate said. "Anyway, it won't happen again."

"There's no need to apologize, Nate," Captain Quincy assured him. "There was no real harm done. Just please, the next time you decide to take off, let someone know."

"Sure, Cap'n."

"There's no harm done as long as these two don't catch their death of pneumonia, bein' in those soaked clothes for who knows how long," Jim said. "Nate, Hoot, you two had better get out of those wet duds. Carl, throw some more wood on the fire. Dan, get 'em some hot coffee."

While Dan went for the coffee, and Carl the wood, Nate and Hoot went to their bunks. When they sat down to take off their boots, they discovered the wet footgear was almost impossible to remove. They had to enlist the help of Ken and Shad to pull off the boots. When Shad gave a tug on Nate's right boot, it came off suddenly, with a dull pop. Shad landed on his backside, still holding the boot and cursing.

"Looks like young Nate, there, done give you the boot, Shad," Joe said, with a chuckle.

"I'll give *him* the boot," Shad retorted.

"I don't want to hear you kickin' about what just happened, Shad," Joe shot back.

Nate and Hoot stripped to the skin, wrapped themselves in blankets, and went back to the stove. They moved two chairs even closer to it and sat down, stretching their legs toward the stove. Dan came back with two steaming mugs of coffee.

"Here you go, boys," he said, handing Nate and Hoot

the hot, black brew. "George added a dollop of whiskey. He said that'll help drive the chill from your bones."

"Thanks, Dan," Hoot said, as he took a mug.

"Yeah, thanks," Nate added. He took a good-sized swallow of the whiskey-laced coffee.

"Dan, this tastes just fine," he said. "It should warm me up real fast."

"Yep, it sure does hit the spot," Hoot added. "It's warmin' my belly up just great." He took another gulp, then wriggled his bare toes. "Boy howdy, that fire sure feels good," he said. "It's gettin' downright cozy in here. I'm real comfortable. Nate, the next time you want to go play in the snow, you're on your own. I'm a southern boy, bred and raised, and I'll take the blazin' hot sun over snow and cold any day, thank you very much."

"You mean you don't want to ride out again tomorrow, Hoot?" Nate asked.

"Only if it's seventy degrees, the sun is shinin', the birds are singin', and the flowers are bloomin'," Hoot answered.

"Nate, do you mind if I ask you a question?" Captain Quincy said.

"Not at all, Cap'n," Nate answered. "What is it?"

"Like Hoot said, he's a southern boy. All of us here are. That means we don't know a whole lot about how to handle cold weather, ice and snow, and all that. In fact, a few years back, up in the Panhandle, I lost a couple of good Rangers to the cold. They got caught in a storm, tried to make it back, but froze to death, less than a quarter mile from town. They were found still holdin' onto their horses' reins. The horses were frozen solid, too. I'm hopin' mebbe you can give us some ideas how to cope with weather like this."

"I'd be glad to, Cap'n," Nate said. "First of all, cover every bit of flesh you can. You don't want frostbite to set in. A man can lose fingers, toes, even a hand or foot from frostbite. If his skin is turning gray, and he's lost all feelin', get him inside, quick. Shiverin's also a bad sign, but a man who's stopped shiverin' is in even worse trouble. You need to get him into a warm place as fast as you can."

"Anythin' special you can do for an hombre who's that far gone?"

"Get him under blankets, near a fire or stove, or in a tub of hot water if one's available. Some folks like to rub a frostbitten man's arms or legs. With luck, any of those will warm him up before it's too late."

"Nate, you said cover every bit of flesh," Jim said. "How about stayin' dry?"

"That's real important, too," Nate answered. "Even wearin' too many clothes can give a man a chill, if he starts sweatin' and those clothes get damp. And of course, a man workin' in the cold will build up a sweat a lot faster'n one just sittin' a horse, or ridin' in a wagon."

"Which is a lesson you and Hoot just forgot," Jeb pointed out.

"I reckon you're right about that, Jeb," Nate admitted.

"Nate, suppose a man's caught out in a storm, and can't get to a warm shelter?" Captain Quincy asked. "Is there anythin' he can do to mebbe save his life?"

"There's a few things," Nate answered. "First, get out of the wind, if possible. Second, if there's enough snow, dig a snow cave. Believe it or not, buryin' yourself under the snow helps keep you warm. And you can still breathe under there, as long as you dig yourself a space around your mouth and nose. You have to make certain the snow

50

doesn't get too packed around you, or you could suffocate. I don't know if any of you have ever seen a picture of the igloos the Eskimos up north build, but a snow cave's the same idea. If you're in the woods, and there's evergreens, you can cut off some branches to build a rough shelter. Evergreen boughs make fine shelters from the snow."

"Is there any way to warm up if you do catch a chill?" Quincy asked.

"You can tuck your hands under your armpits," Nate said. "You can curl up in a ball. If you've got a dog with you, lie down with him up against you. If you're on horseback, get your horse down, and get up against him."

"I heard tell of a feller one time who saved himself durin' a wicked snowstorm by slaughterin' a steer, cuttin' its belly open, and crawlin' inside. The hide froze, but by the time the storm blew over, that feller was still nice and toasty inside that steer's belly," Shad said. "I reckon it'd work with a horse, too, but I sure ain't ever gonna kill my Brandy horse just to save my own skin. If that ever happens, me'n Brandy'll die together."

"I'd reckon a lot of men feel the same way," Jeb said. "I know I do, about my Dudley."

"There is one other way to save a freezin' man's life," Nate said. "Two of my cousins were out huntin' when they got caught by surprise in a wicked storm, and they had to do this. You take the man who's freezin', strip him to the skin, and get him between two blankets. Then the other man, the one who's not dyin' from the cold, also strips to the skin, and slides under the blankets. He's gotta get right up against the first man. His body heat will warm up the dyin' feller, and maybe save his life."

"That seems a mite drastic, Nate," Carl said.

"It is, but it my cousin Martin saved his brother Ned by

doin' just that," Nate answered.

"It wouldn't be so bad, if it was Lily from the Cannon Saloon back in Austin warmin' me up," Joe said. "In fact, it might be worth nearly freezin' to death just to get her alongside me."

"The last time you even tried talkin' to her, Joe, she tossed your beer in your face," Dan answered, laughing, "I'd imagine she'd let you freeze rather'n help you."

"Nate, when you have the time, would you mind writin' up everythin' you just told us for me?" Captain Quincy requested. "I'd like to pass these suggestions along to Headquarters. Someday, they just might save a Ranger's life."

"I'd be glad to," Nate said. He yawned and stretched. "Guess I'm more tuckered out than I realized."

"Cap'n, I reckon the best thing for these two boys right now is a nap," Jeb suggested.

"I can't think of a better idea than that at the moment," Hoot said.

"All right, boys," Captain Quincy said. "Rest a spell. We'll call you when it's time to eat."

The other men returned to their bunks, reading, or card games.

"Hoot," Nate said a few minutes later, "I'm gettin' downright comfortable. Not hardly cold at all, now."

"Yeah, this ain't half bad," Hoot agreed. "The only thing that'd warm me up faster is snugglin' with Clarissa. And I'd say cuddlin' with Consuela, that Mexican firebrand of yours, would heat up a feller real fast. Yessir, real fast."

"Except they're both up at the main house, and we're stuck here, with only each other," Nate said. "More's the shame."

"Yeah, it's a real pity." Hoot shook his head. "A real

pity. Too bad there's nothin' we can do about it. Might as well get some shut-eye." He leaned back and closed his eyes.

"Well, maybe we can at least dream about those girls," Nate said, once again yawning. "That's what I'm gonna do." His eyes shut, and a moment later he was softly snoring.

4

Early the next morning, Nate got out his sketch pad and pencils. He'd decided he wanted to do some drawings of the Circle Dot E while snow still covered the land. Unlike in Delaware, where most winters the ground would be snow-covered from late November or early December through March, here in Texas snow was usually melted away within a few days. He got Big Red, saddled and bridled him, and rode to the top of a low mesa which overlooked the ranch.

"You stay here while I draw, Red," he ordered the sorrel. Red snorted, and commenced nibbling at the tender branches of a scrub willow, which had sprouted from a crack in the rocks. The little tree had somehow found enough moisture to survive. Nate found a rock, brushed the snow off it, sat down, and began to draw.

The Circle Dot E buildings, unlike most in the region, were not constructed of adobe bricks and stucco, but had been built of cedar logs, freighted in at considerable expense. The main house was a low, rambling structure, with a porch across its entire front. The rich, reddish tones of the cedar houses, barns, and outbuildings contrasted nicely against the blinding white snow and the deep azure sky. The pencils seemed to come alive in Nate's hands, as he sketched the buildings, corrals, and yard.

Red wandered over to Nate and nuzzled the back of his neck, then lipped at the sketch pad. He pulled the pencil out of Nate's hand, held it between his lips, and tossed his head.

"You tryin' to tell me you want to go home already, Red?" Nate asked the horse. "I'm not done here, yet."

Red shook his head and snorted.

"I told you we're not goin' back yet," Nate said. He looked at the horse and rubbed his jaw. "Wait a minute. I just thought of somethin'. I've never done a drawin' of you, pal. I'm gonna take care of that right now."

Nate took the pencil from Red, replaced it in his kit and took out another one, then began to draw his horse. The sorrel's rich red coat seemed to glow like a newly-minted copper penny against the backdrop of snow-covered rocks and bright blue, cloudless sky.

"Too bad these pencils are just charcoal, Red, rather'n oil paints," Nate said. "I'd love to have a color paintin' of you. Mebbe someday. But, I sure can't try'n do any oils while I'm ridin' with the Rangers. Canvases, brushes, and oil paints would just take up too much room, and oils take too long to dry. I guess I'll just have to settle for this picture."

In a short time, Nate finished the sketch, and held it up for Red's approval.

"There. You like it?" he asked.

Red nickered, then nuzzled Nate's shirt pocket.

"I get it," Nate said. "You like the drawin', but you'd rather have a piece of biscuit. Well, I've got somethin' even better for you. Stole it outta the cook shack while George wasn't lookin'."

He pulled a carrot from his pocket and gave it to the horse. Red crunched down happily on it.

"Satisfied? Good," Nate said. "I only want to do one more drawing from up here, then we'll head back down. All right?"

Red's only answer was taking another bite off the carrot.

◆●◆

Nate finished his drawing from the mesa top, then headed back down to the ranch proper. He put Big Red back in the corral, forked him some hay, and began to sketch the Circle Dot E's main bunkhouse. Zack Ellesio came out and spotted him.

"What're you up to, Nate?" he asked.

"Just doin' some drawin'," Nate answered. "I like to do that whenever I get the chance."

"Can I take a look?"

"Sure." Nate turned the pad so Zack could see the drawing.

"Say, that's pretty good," Zack praised. "Would you mind drawin' a picture of me and my horse?"

"Not at all," Nate answered.

"Good. Let me go get Shenandoah and I'll be right back," Zack said. He hurried toward the main stable.

Nate put the last details on his sketch of the bunkhouse while he waited for Zack to return. The young cowboy took longer than he expected, so Nate did another drawing, of several saddles hung on the top rail of the corral, to keep busy until Zack got back. He was nearly finished with that one before Zack reappeared.

"Sorry I took so long, Nate," Zack apologized, "But I wanted to get Shenandoah all slicked up, and put my fancy, go-to-town saddle blanket on him."

"That's all right, Zack," Nate answered. "There's plenty

here for me to draw while I was waitin', and you did a fine job on your horse. It's just too bad these are only pencil sketches. That's a right pretty saddle blanket your horse is wearin', and I'd have loved to do a color paintin' for you. You're lookin' pretty fancy, too."

Zack had brushed his chestnut gelding so that even his thick winter coat shone like a chunk of raw copper. The horse's mane and tail were combed out, and he sported a colorful Navajo patterned blanket under his saddle. Zack had even polished the silver conchos on Shenandoah's bridle. And the young cowboy had also brushed the dirt off his sweat-stained hat, changed into a clean yellow shirt, and hung a bright green silk bandanna around his neck.

"That don't matter none, as long as I can have a picture of me'n Shenandoah," Zack answered.

"That, you'll have," Nate assured him. "How do you want to be drawn? Standin' next to your horse or sittin' on him?"

"I'd rather be in the saddle," Zack replied. "Can you do the picture with me holdin' my gun in my hand, like I'm gettin' ready to shoot some outlaw?"

"Sure, that'll be easy," Nate said. "Just climb on up there."

"All right."

Zack mounted his horse, pulled out his six-gun, leveled it, and screwed up his face into a look of grim determination, almost a scowl.

"Do I look mean enough, Nate?" he asked.

"That's almost as mean as the look you gave me the day you found me," Nate answered. "It's enough to scare the bejeebers out of pretty much anyone. Now, stay as still as you can. Hold Shenandoah as quiet as you can keep him, too. I'll do a quick sketch, then fill in the details.

Your arm'd get too tired holdin' that gun up long enough for me to finish the whole drawin'."

"Sure thing, Nate."

Nate rapidly drew, and soon a rough image of Zack and his horse appeared on the paper.

"You can put your gun away now, Zack, but stay up there a bit longer," he said. "I want to get a few more details before you get down."

"All right, Nate. I'll stay in the saddle as long as I need to, for a picture."

Several other Circle Dot E hands, having been told by Zack what Nate was up to, had come out of the bunkhouse, and watched as Nate sketched.

"You mind doin' a picture of me, Nate?" Justin Bendlak, a young cowboy about Zack's age, requested. "I'd sure be pleased to have one."

"Me, too, if you can?" Nicolas Pearson, another young waddy, added.

"I'd like one of me with that sorrel colt I'm tryin' to break," Hunt Knudsen, the ranch's head wrangler, said.

"Sure, I'll do as many as I can before the light's gone," Nate said. "These are just quick sketches, so they won't be as nice, or have as much detail, as a real painting, but you'll sure be able to recognize yourselves. I promise you that."

"I dunno. That drawin' you've got there of Zack seems pretty darn good to me," Hunt said. "How about you fellers?"

The other men murmured their agreement, and nodded.

"All right then," Nate said. "I'll be done with Zack's picture shortly. Justin, I'll do yours next. Why don't you fellers figure out what you want to wear, change clothes if you need to, then come back here? Think on how you want to pose, too."

"We'll do that. Be back quick as we can," Justin answered. He and the other men went back to the bunkhouse, while Nate continued penciling in the final details of Zack's portrait.

◆●◆

Nate spent most of the day drawing pictures of any of the Circle Dot E hands who wanted one. The crew was a mixture of men of almost all ages, races, and backgrounds. There were young men looking for adventure, as well as veteran hands. About half of the men were white, a third Mexican, the rest blacks—most of those, former slaves. It turned out almost every man did ask for a drawing, so Nate only took a break for his noon time dinner, then got back to work. It was about four in the afternoon when Hoot and Clarissa came riding in, Hoot on his horse Sandy, and Clarissa on Slate, a steeldust gray, one of the ranch's horses. They stopped close to where Nate was just completing a sketch of Kyle Newton, another of the spread's cowboys.

"Howdy, Nate. What're you up to?" Hoot asked.

"Drawin' some pictures of the cowboys around here," Nate answered. "I was wonderin' where you'd gotten yourself off to. I reckon I don't have to ask. Guess the cold doesn't bother you all that much, after all."

"Me'n Clarissa took a ride down to the Rio," Hoot answered. "We took along a picnic lunch. Her ma gave us fried chicken and all the fixin's."

"Kind of chilly for a picnic, ain't it?" Nate asked.

"It was a bit nippy. Good for snugglin', though," Hoot replied. Clarissa leaned over in her saddle and slapped his shoulder.

"Henry Harrison, go on with you!" To Nate, she continued. "Don't believe a word he says. We just took a leisurely ride, ate a nice meal, and watched the river. That's all. And now it's time for me to say good night. My mother and father will be looking for me. We were supposed to return an hour ago."

"Clarissa, before you go back to the house, why don't you let Nate draw a picture of me and you?" Hoot suggested.

"Henry, I'd love that," Clarissa said. "Would you mind, Nate?"

"Not at all, I'd be happy to," Nate answered.

"Wonderful. But I really should let my parents know I'm home," Clarissa answered.

"I can do that for you, Miss Hennessey," Kyle offered. "Nate's just about done with my picture, anyway."

"I keep telling all you boys, my name's Clarissa, not Miss Hennessey," Clarissa answered. "Thank you, Kyle. You're a sweetheart."

"It's no trouble, Miss Hennessey," Kyle answered. "And I'm sorry, but I just can't call you by your first name. You're the boss's daughter. It wouldn't be proper."

"Here's your picture, Kyle." Nate handed him the drawing, which showed Kyle seated on the corral fence, gazing into the distance.

Kyle took the picture, looked at it, and smiled.

"This is just perfect, Nate," he said. "I'm gonna send it to my ma, back in Wichita. She didn't want me to leave home, but I didn't want to spend my life clerkin' in my uncle's store. I wanted to be a cowboy, ridin' the trails and sleepin' under the stars. Never realized cowboyin's mostly hard, dirty work. But I still love it. Anyway, thanks for the picture, Nate. She'll sure be happy to get this."

"*De nada,* Kyle. Hoot, if you and Clarissa are ready, I'll get started on your pictures now. I'm guessin' you'll want two copies... one each," Nate said.

"You guessed right," Hoot answered, with a grin. "Clarissa, I'd kinda like to have this picture showin' us settin' on our horses, if that's all right with you."

"Of course it is, Henry. Whatever you'd like is fine with me," Clarissa answered.

"Then, let me get started," Nate said. Once Hoot and Clarissa were in place, he began sketching. With the light starting to fade, he worked quickly. He had almost completed the first drawing when Consuela came from the main house.

"*Senorita* Clarissa, supper will be ready in thirty minutes," she said. "Your mother would like you to come up to the house now, so you can clean up and change before the meal."

"Tell her I'll be along in a few minutes, Consuela," Clarissa answered. "Nate has to finish my picture first."

"You can go on ahead, Clarissa," Nate said. "I'm just about done with this one. I'll make a copy of it tonight, and get it to you tomorrow."

"Are you certain, Nate?" she asked.

"I am. I don't need you and Hoot to pose for both copies. I'll just draw another one from this one," Nate explained.

"And I'll put up your horse, so you don't have to worry about him," Hoot added.

"Thank you, Henry." Clarissa leaned over, gave Hoot a kiss on the cheek, and dismounted. She handed her reins to him. "I'll see you tomorrow, I hope."

"As long as we don't have to ride out, I'll be here," Hoot

promised her. "Good night, Clarissa."

"Good night, Henry. Consuela, are you walking back to the house with me?"

"You go without me, *Senorita* Clarissa," Consuela answered. "I need to speak with Nate for a moment. Tell your *madre* I'll be along in time to serve supper."

"Of course. I understand." Clarissa gave her a knowing smile. "I'll see you at the house."

"You wanted to talk to me, Consuela?" Nate asked.

"Didn't I just say that?" Consuela answered, her voice petulant.

"Yeah, I reckon you did," Nate answered. "What's wrong? You sound a bit upset."

"Wrong, Nate? Whatever gave you that idea?" Consuela retorted. "Nothing's wrong. I'm not the least bit angry. Just because you promised me days ago that you would draw my picture, which you haven't gotten around to yet, and now I find you drawing pictures of everyone on the ranch but me, why should I be angry?"

"Consuela, I'm sorry," Nate tried to apologize. "I didn't plan this. I was sketching some of the ranch buildings, when Zack asked if I'd draw his picture. I didn't know just about every hombre on the place would show up, wanting their pictures done too. I'll draw you tomorrow, I promise."

"I don't believe you," Consuela snapped. "I want you to draw my picture, right now."

"I can't," Nate said. "The light's getting too dim. And don't you have to get back to help serve the Hennesseys' supper?"

"That has nothing to do with this, Nate."

"I don't want to see you get in trouble on my account, just because I forgot to do your picture," Nate answered. "I'll tell you what. After supper, once your work is done, why don't you meet me back here? We can go in the barn, and I'll sketch you by lantern light."

"I'm not certain," Consuela answered, hesitating. "I really shouldn't."

"Please, Consuela," Nate said. "The soft light from the lantern will be very flattering. You'll look beautiful."

"I'm still not sure. It wouldn't be... Oh, all right." Consuela gave in. "I'll meet you at seven-thirty, unless *Senora* Louella has more chores for me."

"Great. I'll see you then." Nate gave her a quick peck on the cheek.

"Pretty smooth, pard," Hoot said to Nate, once Consuela was out of earshot. He nudged him in the ribs. "Convincin' her to meet you at the barn, after dark. Where it'll be just you and her, alone. Just the two of you. With all that nice, soft hay."

Nate punched Hoot on the arm.

"Hey, I'm just gonna draw her picture, that's all," he protested. "I told her I would, days ago."

"Sure you are. And all me and Clarissa did was watch the river, Nate. No cuddlin' at all," Hoot said. "Now, you want to give me a hand with these horses?"

"I reckon I can do that...*Henry*," Nate answered, chuckling. Hoot thumped him in the stomach.

"Nobody calls me Henry."

"Except Clarissa...*Henry*," Nate said, still laughing.

"Well, the day you're as pretty as her, and have curves in the same places she does, Nate, then you can call me Henry, too," Hoot said. "Until then, my name's Hoot, and don't you forget it. Now, let's get these animals put up."

◆●◆

During supper, Nate sketched a few pictures of the

Rangers as they ate, then excused himself by saying Red had a cut he wanted to check, and left for the barn. He waited anxiously, until there was a gentle knock on the closed door.

"Nate? Are you in there?" Consuela softly called.

"Yeah, I am. C'mon in."

Nate slid the door open, just wide enough for Consuela to slip through, then closed it behind her.

"I'm glad you came, Consuela," he said.

"I nearly didn't. And I'm still not certain I should have," Consuela answered. "I'm sorry I'm a bit late, but I had to help *Senora* Louella with some mending. You'll do this drawing as quickly as possible, won't you? I don't want to be missed at the house."

"Of course I will," Nate promised her.

"*Gracias*, Nate. Where would you like me to be?"

"On that bench over there, between the two lanterns," Nate said. "The light's just about right, and I figure it'll be the most comfortable spot for you, since you'll have to stay as still as possible while I draw."

"All right. If you're ready, I'd like to get started," Consuela said. "Like I said, I'm still not really comfortable doing this. It just doesn't seem right. Perhaps I should have said no, or at least brought along *Senorita* Claire or *Senorita* Clarissa, so we would not be alone."

"I'm just waitin' for you to get in place," Nate answered. "And there's nothin' to worry about. I'm just gonna draw your picture."

Consuela walked over to the bench, then removed the heavy, dark wool shawl she wore. Nate gasped when she turned, and showed him her outfit.

"Consuela... you're, you're beautiful!" he exclaimed.

"Why, *muchas gracias*, *Senor* Nate," she said, giving

him a demure smile. "I am glad you think so."

Consuela was clad in a fairly low cut white blouse, with lace trim on its bodice, and a flowing, multi-colored striped skirt. A mother-of-pearl *mantilla* held her long, black hair in place. In the soft light of the lanterns, that hair resembled an ebony waterfall.

"I've never seen you dressed like that," Nate said.

"That's because you've only seen me when I'm working," Consuela answered. "Now, shall we begin?" She sat down, smoothed her skirt, tilted her head slightly, and smiled at Nate. That smile took his breath away.

"Yeah. Yeah, I reckon we should," Nate said. He picked up his pad and a pencil, and began to draw. Despite the chill in the air, his face seemed flushed, and he felt a warmth clear down to his toes. "I'm gonna do a couple drawings, if you don't mind," he said. "One for me, one for you."

"That's just fine, Nate," Consuela said. She sat, motionless, only the soft heaving of her bosom indicating she was even alive, as he drew. Nate quickly dashed off one picture, had her change her pose slightly, then drew another.

"We're finished, Consuela," he said, as he tore the pages from his pad, and handed them to her. "Choose which one you like best. I'll take the other one."

Consuela took the drawings, and looked at them for a moment.

"Nate, these are wonderful. They're perfect," she said. "I love them both. I can't decide right now. Would you mind if I took them both with me, so I can see them in the morning light, then choose? I'll bring back whichever one I decide not to keep."

"Of course," Nate answered. "You can keep both of

them, if you'd like."

"No. Then you wouldn't have one of me, and I want you to have my picture, to keep with you as you ride," Consuela said. "And perhaps some day you can draw one of yourself, for me."

"I'd crack a mirror if I looked in one to do that," Nate answered, with a laugh.

"No, you would not. Not at all," Consuela said. "You really are quite handsome. Now, I really should return to the house, before I am missed. *Buenas noches*, Nate."

She lifted her face to Nate, and gave him a quick kiss. Before he even realized what he was doing, Nate had his arms wrapped around her. He returned the kiss, eagerly, then pushed himself away.

"I-I'm sorry, Consuela. I didn't—I mean, I shouldn't..."

"Shh." Consuela touched a finger to his lips. "It's all right, Nate. I liked your kiss. Perhaps..." She left the sentence unfinished. Instead, she pulled him to her, and kissed him once again. She put a hand on his neck, and held his face to hers for a long, lingering kiss. They fell back on the bench.

"Nate," she said, softly.

"Don't say anything," Nate answered. "You don't need to say a word." He pressed his lips to hers, holding her tightly. He began to run his hand down her back, but stopped at the sound of rapidly approaching horses.

"Riders!" he exclaimed.

"Riders?" Consuela echoed. Her eyes grew wide with fear.

"Yeah. Comin' in fast," Nate said. "And at this time of the night, it can only mean one thing...trouble." He pulled the gun from his holster. "You stay here until I see what they're after. Better yet, get up in the loft, and stay there, until I'm certain it's safe."

"Nate..."

"Do it, now!" Nate snapped. Consuela ran down the aisle and scrambled up the ladder, into the hayloft. Nate waited until he was certain she was out of sight, then slid open the barn door, just enough so he could look out over the moon-covered landscape. The shadowy figures of several horsemen, just cresting the rise overlooking the Circle Dot E, were rapidly approaching. Nate squinted, attempting to make out their features in the dim light of a just rising crescent moon. As the riders drew nearer, he could see there were three of them. They reached the bottom of the hill and rode straight for the Circle Dot E's main house.

"Consuela, they're headed for the house," Nate whispered. "You stay hidden, until I figure out what they're up to."

"All right," Consuela answered, "but be careful, Nate."

"I'll do my best," Nate said. He slipped out the door, and started for the house. He noticed Captain Quincy, Jim, and Dan emerge from the Rangers' bunkhouse.

Clearly, the rest of the Rangers had also heard the riders, and Captain Quincy would not let them go unchallenged. Nate smiled when he realized only those three men were going to leave their quarters. That was another lesson he'd learned from Captain Quincy. Never show every card in your hand until you had a good idea what the other feller was holding.

The captain was obviously leaving the rest of his men in reserve, in case of real trouble. At the main bunkhouse, Nate knew, the ranch hands would also be on alert for trouble, and even now most likely already had several guns trained on the newcomers.

The three men reached the house and dismounted. One held the reins of their horses, while the other two stepped onto the porch and knocked on the door. Nate could make out a bit of their faces by the light from the lanterns hung on each side of the door.

Another bad sign, Nate thought. *If those hombres weren't in a hurry, they'd have tied their horses and all three gone into the house.*

Charlie Hennessey, holding a Winchester in his hand, answered the knock. Behind him, Nate could see his son Brian, also holding a rifle. Brian's was already pointed at the strangers, while Hennessey held his at his side, ready to swing up and put into action at the first sign of trouble.

"Can I help you men?" Hennessey asked. His voice drifted to Nate through the still night air.

"Mebbe," one of the men answered. "We're trailin' a couple of *hombres* we figure might have come this way. We were gainin' on 'em, until the storm hit night before last. We had to hole up until it blew over. By then, all their tracks were wiped out, but this is pretty much the only way they could have gone, unless they got lost, and are lyin' in the brush somewhere, froze to death. You had anybody come by this way?"

"That depends," Hennessey answered. "First, I want to know why you're after these men. Do you mind tellin' me that?"

"I reckon that's none of your business, mister," the second rider said. "Quit wastin' our time. You gonna tell us if those men are here or not?"

"Not until you answer my question," Hennessey answered. He lifted his rifle and pointed it at the nearest man.

"Lower that gun and get outta our way, mister," the

first man ordered. "You're interferin' with the law."

Captain Quincy and the men with him, as well as Nate, who was now with them, had stopped just beyond the circle of lamplight. Quincy's voice sliced through the night like a knife.

"Any trouble here, Mr. Hennessey? We can take care of it if we need to. There's four guns pointin' at those *hombres* right now. Just say the word and we'll drop 'em right where they stand."

The three riders, startled, caught unawares, with their guns still holstered, jerked around at the sound of Quincy's voice. The man holding the horses tried to slip a rifle from its scabbard. Quincy put a bullet into the ground between his feet.

"Try that again and the next one's through your belly, mister," the captain warned. "Now, you get up on the porch with your friends. All three of you, drop your guns, then raise your hands. No false moves. Remember, there's four guns pointed right at your middles."

"He's got the drop on us, Mal," the horse holder said, as he stepped onto the porch, unbuckled his gunbelt, and let it fall. He companions followed his lead.

"Don't worry, Fred," the apparent leader answered. "We'll get this all straightened out in a minute, once we can explain to these men why we're here." To Hennessey, he said, "Mind if we come inside and palaver? It's right cold out here, and we've been ridin' all day."

"We'll handle this, Charlie," Captain Quincy said, as he stepped into the light with his men on either side of him. "Y'all just stand hitched," he ordered. "We can talk right here. I heard you claim you were lawmen."

"That's right," the leader answered. "I'm Deputy Sheriff Malcolm Prentiss. My pardners are Deputies Fred Hayes and Jesus Montalban. We're out of *Dona Ana* County, over to New Mexico Territory. We've been trailin' two wanted outlaws."

"You're a bit out of your jurisdiction, deputy," Quincy answered. "Just so you know who you're dealin' with, I'm Captain David Quincy of the Texas Rangers. These men are Rangers Kelly, Morton, and Stewart. Now, I don't know how you do things up in New Mexico, but here in Texas, we generally frown on people who go bustin' into innocent folks' homes without a good reason."

"We've got a good reason," Prentiss answered. "I told you, we're after two wanted men. Now, as Rangers, if you've seen those men, you can help us find 'em, and turn 'em over to us, all nice and legal-like."

"Who you have no idea might be in this house, except they headed in this direction," Quincy answered. "And we're sure not gonna help you unless you give us a good reason. You can start by givin' us their names."

"Those men are killers," Prentiss answered. "They go by the names of Curly Thomas and Deke Vance. They gunned down four men in cold blood, at a saloon just outside Las Cruces."

"I assume you've got proof of that. And also proof of your identities," Quincy answered.

"Sure we do, Ranger. But could you at least tell us if you've seen those men?" Prentiss said.

"Charlie, what were the names of those men who rode in here just ahead of the storm?" Quincy asked.

"Thomas and Vance," Hennessey answered. "They claimed they were lookin' for jobs. My foreman told 'em we weren't hirin', but that they could stay here for a few days, to rest themselves and their horses. They're in the bunkhouse right now, I'd imagine. At least, I haven't seen 'em ride out."

"There, you see, Ranger. Those men *are* here," Prentiss said. "Now, we'll just take them off your hands."

"Not quite so fast, Prentiss," Quincy said. "You seem awful eager to get your hands on those *hombres*."

"Of course we are, Ranger," Montalban said. "We've been on their trail for a long time, and want to get home. Now, can we have them?"

"Not yet," Quincy answered. "I want to hear their side of the story first. And, of course, you *do* have warrants, as well as extradition papers, signed by the Governor of Texas, right? Jim, Nate, go get Thomas and Vance, and bring them here. Be careful, just in case they try to make a run for it."

"Right away, Cap'n," Jim said.

"Prentiss, just in case you've forgotten, there's still four guns trained on you," Quincy reminded the deputy. "Two here, and two from the doorway. So just stay nice and quiet until my men get back."

"You're makin' a big mistake, if you think those *hombres* are anythin' but sneakin', back-shootin' murderers," Hayes said.

"Mebbe," Quincy admitted. "But let's just see what they have to say for themselves."

The deputies continued to mutter under their breaths, threatening what they would do if their quarry escaped, with curses directed at the Hennesseys and the Rangers. Jim and Nate returned with their six-guns pointed at the unarmed Thomas's and Vance's backs, as the men walked in front of them, hands in the air. They'd ordered the Circle Dot E hands to stay in the bunkhouse. The cowboys chafed at the order, and grumbled, but remained inside.

"That's them, Ranger," Prentiss shouted. "That's the

ones who gunned down four innocent men by shootin' 'em in the back."

"So, you finally caught up to us, Prentiss," Thomas said. "We we're hopin' you'd quit chasin' us, and be satisfied with keepin' the horses you stole from us. I reckon we should've known better. You can't take a chance on leavin' us alive. And what he just told you's a baldfaced lie, Ranger," he said to Quincy. "We did have to shoot four men. But it was a fair fight, and all of 'em took bullets from the front, in their chests or bellies. Not one of 'em was drilled in the back."

"Stop tryin' to worm your way out of this, Thomas," Prentiss growled. "Ranger, you just heard him admit he and his pardner did those killin's. So, why don't you just turn 'em over to us, and we'll be on our way."

"Not until we hear the rest of what they have to say," Quincy answered. "Their version of what happened seems to be a bit different than yours. Thomas, finish your story. These men claim to be deputies from *Dona Ana* County. Is that right?"

"It is," Thomas admitted. "Although they're no honest lawmen, despite what they might claim. Me'n Deke had been up to Santa Fe, checkin' on some horses we heard might make good breedin' stock. They were real fine animals, so we made a deal for some of 'em. We was drivin' 'em back home to San Angelo. When we came through Las Cruces, Prentiss, there, tried to claim we'd stolen the horses, even though we had bills of sale for the entire bunch. He let us go, since with our papers provin' we'd bought those horses he couldn't make his charges stick—or so we'd thought, but it turns out he and some of his men followed us. When we bedded down for the night, him and his bunch jumped us. We managed to down four of 'em, but there were too many for us. They drove off our stock, and nearly got us, too. I've got the bullet slash along my ribs to prove it, if you need to see it. We got away, and figured there was no chance of ever seein' those horses again, let alone get 'em back. Me'n Deke decided we'd better cut our losses, although losin' those horses meant we were wiped out, and get back to Texas with our hides in one piece, at least."

"That's a lie," Prentiss shouted. "Ranger, he's lyin'. Him and his pardner shot four men over a card game. They murdered 'em, pure and simple."

"That just not so, and you know it, Prentiss," Vance said, quietly. "Ranger, I've still got the bill of sale for those cayuses in my saddlebags, if you'd like to see it."

"I believe I would," Quincy said.

"You're gonna take the word of a killer and horse thief over mine, Ranger?" Prentiss objected.

"Unless you can prove otherwise, I don't believe these men are killers and horse thieves," Quincy answered. "You haven't shown me one shred of evidence against 'em. Now, since Thomas has confirmed you are deputies, I don't need to see your badges or papers, but I sure would like to see the warrant charging these men, and the extradition papers."

"We didn't bring a warrant. Didn't figure we'd need one," Prentiss said. "As far as those, what'd you call 'em, extradition papers, I don't even know what the devil those are. But these men are wanted back in New Mexico, and we figure on takin' 'em there."

"No warrants, and no extradition papers." Quincy removed his Stetson, ran a hand through his hair, then replaced the hat and rubbed his jaw. "That means you have no evidence against these men, no legal authority to

73

arrest them, and no authority from the State of Texas orderin' me to turn them over to you. So, I'd say you'd best leave, right now, before you get yourselves into any further trouble. There are no charges against you three in Texas, at least none that I know of, but unless you get outta here—and I mean right now—you can be dang certain I'll come up with some. So pick up your guns, and git!"

"You ain't heard the last of this, Ranger," Prentiss said, adding a curse for good measure.

"I'd better have," Quincy answered, waggling his gun for emphasis. "Now, get goin'."

Still muttering curses, the three New Mexico lawmen picked up their guns, then their horses' reins. Once off the porch, Prentiss nodded, almost imperceptibly, to his partners. Without warning, they dove to the ground behind their horses, and began shooting.

"Rangers, Mr. Hennessey, look out!" Thomas shouted, needlessly, for the Rangers were already in action, as were Hennessey and his son. A bullet tore the air just over Nate's head, another plucked at Dan's shirt, but the gun battle was over almost as quickly as it started. The deputies' panicked horses galloped off, leaving behind their riders, who were lying in the snow, bullet riddled. The snow was tinged red, fading to rose, then pink, by their blood.

"Everyone all right?" Quincy asked.

"Seem to be," Jim said.

"Except one of those sidewinders put a hole through my favorite shirt!" Dan answered, adding a few choice curse words for emphasis.

"Same here," Hennessey added. "We're fine. Brian, go tell your mother and the rest of the family no one got hurt, except for those so-called deputies." He spat in the direction of the dead men.

"All right, Pa."

"Dan, you go tell the men everythin's under control," Quincy ordered. "Nate, you pass the same word to the cowboys."

"We're on our way," Dan answered.

"Ranger, me'n Curly are plumb grateful for what you just did," Vance said to Quincy. "Those men would've killed us before we'd gone a mile."

"*De nada,*" Quincy answered. "I figured they were lyin', the moment I laid eyes on 'em. Sometimes, you just know. It's an instinct a lawman develops. Well, I reckon I've got to write up a report for Austin. Charlie, if you could take care of the bodies, once I check them for personal effects..."

"Sure thing, Cap'n. There's a spot down along the creek where the ground won't be frozen, at least not too deep. We'll put 'em in the shed overnight and plant 'em in the mornin'."

"That'll do," Quincy said. "Thomas, Vance," he continued, "if I understood you correctly, losin' those horses has pretty much wiped you out. Am I right?"

"You are," Thomas confirmed. "We spent almost all our savin's on those broncs."

"Well, I can't help with that, but if you'd like to consider it, I could use a couple more men," Quincy said. "The pay ain't much, the food's lousy, and you'll always be lookin' for the hombre who's tryin' to put a bullet in your back, but if you think you'd like to give Rangerin' a try, I'll take a chance, and sign you both on."

"Why, thanks, Cap'n," Thomas said. "What d'ya think, Deke?"

"I say why not?" Vance answered. "Bein' as we don't

have any other prospects."

"All right. Cap'n, it looks like you've just signed yourself up two new recruits," Thomas said.

"Good. Since you're already settled for the night, you can move your stuff to the bunkhouse we're usin' come mornin'. We'll do the paperwork and swear you in then. Now, I guess that's enough excitement for one night. I'm ready for some shut-eye."

◆●◆

Once Nate had told the ranch hands what had happened, he headed for the stable on the run. As soon as he stepped inside, Consuela threw herself into his arms.

"Oh, Nate, Nate," she cried, weeping softly. "I was watching from the hayloft, and saw everything that happened. I was so frightened for you."

"It's all right, Consuela," Nate reassured her, stroking her hair. "I wasn't hurt. No one was, except those riders."

"Who were they?" Consuela asked.

"Deputies from New Mexico, lookin' for a couple of men. Turns out, the deputies were the crooked ones, and the men they were after weren't," Nate answered. "I'll tell you all about it tomorrow. Right now, you'd better get back to the house, before you're missed."

"The house! You're right, Nate," Consuela exclaimed. "*Senora* Louella will be looking for me. I need to return, right now."

"*Manana, mi corazon.*"

She gave Nate a quick kiss on the cheek, then disappeared into the night.

5

Like practically everything about Texas, the changes in weather were often extreme, a fitting match for the vast land which was the Lone Star State. February turned into March, and memories of the blizzard and extreme cold faded as the weather grew warmer, migrating birds returned, and flowers burst into bloom. Mother Nature seemed to ignore the calendar, skipping straight from spring to summer, as she replaced snow, ice, and frigid temperatures with summer-like heat. On the Circle Dot E ranch, some of the cows had already dropped their spring calves, and most of the mares were heavy with foal. Several chuckline riding cowboys had already shown up at the ranch, looking for work.

The Rangers knew they would have to leave the comfortable quarters they'd had for the past three months soon, since the spare bunkhouse would be needed for the hands hired for the spring and summer work. They'd kept patrolling the Big Bend area over the rest of the winter, making a few arrests, but more often than not frustrated in trying to round up the outlaws plaguing the territory. It was like hunting for gophers. You'd find one, but as soon as you caught one three more would pop up. However, their presence did seem to have some effect. Reports of robberies, cattle rustling, and horse thievery were down sharply. Captain Quincy still wasn't certain whether that was due to the presence of the Rangers, or the bad weather. If it were the weather, then with the coming of warmer temperatures and dry, sunny days outlaws would start their depredations once again.

This God-forsaken corner of Texas was extremely isolated, so much so that the telegraph lines had not yet reached Presidio. Two weeks previously, Captain Quincy had sent a letter to Austin, asking if his company would be reassigned to another area of the state, or would remain in the Big Bend. If it were the latter, then they would have to move soon, probably to reestablish their camp along Blue Creek. It was just a matter of waiting for the reply to come, on the once weekly stage. He had stationed Ken Demarest and Phil Knight in Presidio, to await Headquarters' response. While they were waiting, the pair would help the Presidio town marshal to maintain order, and also patrol the surrounding area.

Jeb's patrol returned to the Circle Dot E late in the afternoon on a far hotter than normal day. It had been an exhausting two weeks, while they pursued a band of smugglers who were bringing opium and 'dobe dollars into Texas from Mexico. In the end, they had been unsuccessful.

The smugglers eluded them by swimming their horses across the Rio Grande, then disappearing into the Chihuahan desert. Almost completely spent once they got back, every man in the patrol cared for their horses, ate a quick supper, then tumbled into bed.

The next morning, when Jeb made his report to Captain Quincy and asked for his patrol's next assignment, Quincy told him to, along with his men, just take it easy for the next few days, since he was expecting new orders from Austin anytime now. As all the patrols returned, he was going to keep them in, until he heard from Headquarters.

The next day was even hotter, with temperatures well into the eighties. Consuela had to work all day, so Nate decided to take a ride, then a swim. Unfortunately, when they reached the creek, it had virtually dried up. Where there should have been a swimming hole was a trickle of water, surrounded by mud. Nate muttered in disgust.

"Looks like we just wasted our time, Red," he said to his horse. "I guess we might as well go back to the ranch. We'll just have to clean up as best we can there."

He turned Red away from the creek. When he did, what appeared to be solid ground collapsed under them, sending both sliding down an embankment, into the deep mud. Red sank nearly to his belly, whinnying in fear as he struggled to break free of the sucking goo. Nate left the saddle, and was immediately almost waist deep in mud. He was stuck as effectively as his horse.

"Easy, Red," he tried to sooth his frantic sorrel. "We'll figure a way out of this. Just lemme see."

Nate looked at his surroundings. About fifteen feet away was a solid-looking boulder, small enough to toss his rope around.

"I think I've got it, Red." He lifted the rope from his saddle, shook out a loop, and made his throw. The loop settled around the rock. Nate tugged it until it tightened, then began to pull himself, hand over hand, out of the muck. It was a tedious process, and once he lost his grip, to fall flat on his face, coating himself even more completely with the sticky goo, but gradually, he was able to get free.

"I'm gonna pull you outta there now, boy," he called to

Red. "Just help me out. Don't fight me." He removed his rope from the boulder, shook out another loop, and tossed it at Red. His first try fell short, but the next one fell gently over the sorrel's neck. Nate tightened it, and began to pull. He managed to move Red about two feet, then the horse seemed to bog down even more.

"Try'n help me out here, Red," Nate pleaded. "You've gotta try. I can't pull you free on my own." He began tugging on the rope, yet again. He got Red about a foot closer to solid ground, then the horse appeared to quit struggling.

"Don't you give up, Red!" Nate shouted. "I'm not lettin' you die in that muck, you hear me?" Nonetheless, the situation seemed hopeless. Nate couldn't get enough leverage to wrench his horse free from the grasping ooze. And by the time he was able to walk back for help, it would be too late. Red would have died of exhaustion, or from injuries as he struggled to break free.

"Wait a minute. I've got it, Red," he exclaimed. "I'm gonna get you outta there, pal."

Nate took his rope, wrapped the end around his waist and tied it tight, then looped it around the boulder.

"You'll be out of that mud in a coupla' minutes," Nate promised. Leaning back against the rope tied around his waist and looped around the rock, Nate began to pull, every time he felt slack taking a step or two back to keep the rope taut. At first, any movement was almost imperceptible; but inch by inch, Nate began to pull Red out of the sucking mud. Suddenly, Red gave a lunge, when his front feet hit solid ground, still hidden.

"That's the boy, Red!" Nate shouted encouragement to his horse, while he pulled even harder on the rope. Red's front end was clear, his front hooves clawing for purchase, the muscles in his hindquarters bulging with his frantic efforts to burst free. With a final lunge, he pulled himself out of danger. The rope went slack, and Nate, still leaning against it, fell flat on his back. Red shook himself, walked over to Nate, and nuzzled his face. Nate rubbed the gelding's nose and laughed with relief.

"That was too close for comfort," he said. "Lemme get up, and make sure you're all right."

Nate got up, and checked over Red for any injuries. Despite his struggles, the horse seemed unharmed, although he would undoubtedly have some stiff muscles come morning. So would Nate, for that matter.

"Reckon we were both lucky, horse," he said. "Neither one of us seems that much the worse for wear. Thank the Good Lord Phil taught me how to use a rope."

Nate's clothes, except for his hat, were covered with mud. His six-gun was clogged, and would need to be cleaned thoroughly as soon as he got back to the ranch. But at least he hadn't lost it, nor his boots, for that matter. Somehow, they hadn't been sucked off by the mud, and were still on his feet.

"I guess we'd better get back, and get cleaned up, Red."

Nate recoiled his rope, hung it back from his saddlehorn, and got back on his horse. He put Red into motion. The worn-out gelding, his head hanging low, moved out at a slow walk. Nate murmured a silent prayer of thanks that he, and his horse, had escaped the sticky trap.

◆●◆

"I sure hope we can sneak in without anyone seein' us, Red," Nate said, as they neared the ranch. "I don't want to have to explain what happened."

His hope was short-lived, for when he tried to ride behind the bunkhouse without being spotted, George was there, sitting on an overturned washtub and peeling potatoes for that night's supper. He glanced up when he heard Nate approach.

"Nate! What the devil happened to you, boy?" he yelled.

"Red lost his footing. We fell into a little mud puddle," Nate answered.

"A *little* mud puddle?" George echoed. "More like a mud vat. Or mebbe a mud pond. Or an entire mud lake. Yeah, that's it...a mud lake. I've seen buffaloes come out of wallows, and pigs rootin' around in their sties, covered with less mud than you and your horse. You're dang lucky it wasn't quicksand you got yourself into, or your cayuse would've been sucked right under, and most likely, no one would ever have been able to figure out why you just up and disappeared without a trace. Well, son, it appears like you've got a mite of cleanin' up to do before supper."

"I reckon so," Nate conceded. "A bit more than a mite, in fact. George, you ain't gonna tell any of the other fellers about this, are you? Please?"

"I don't hardly see how I can keep quiet about it," George said, laughing. "It's too good a tale to keep to myself. Besides, there's no way to keep it a secret. You'll never be able to sneak into the bunkhouse, get out of those filthy duds, and wash up before someone sees you. And that's not even mentionin' your horse and gear. No, I figure this story's gonna spread like a prairie wildfire, Nate."

"That's what I was afraid of," Nate answered, miserably. "Well, I guess I'd better get to work."

He dismounted, and led Red inside the stable. He put him in a stall and stripped the gear from him. After giving

82

the sorrel some hay, he found a bucket and several rags. He went out back to the trough and filled the bucket, then came back to Red. While his horse munched on the hay, Nate scrubbed the thick mud from his hide, as best he could. Once that was finished, he took out Red's currycomb and dandy brush. He brushed him thoroughly, then got a hoof pick and cleaned out his hooves.

"I'll turn you out a bit later, Red," Nate promised the horse, with a pat on the shoulder. "Gonna wash some of the mud off your saddle, then try'n clean up myself."

Red nickered, then went back to working on his hay. Nate soaked another rag, and used that to wipe his saddle. Luckily, except for a few splatters, it was mostly the fenders, stirrups, and cinch straps which were thickly coated with dried mud. Even the saddle blanket sported only a few spots. Nate took that to wash in the trough, then drape over the fence to dry.

Once his horse and gear were cared for, Nate turned his attention to himself. He decided not to go into the bunkhouse washroom to clean up, since that would leave a trail of mud through the entire building, and dirt he would have to clean up all over the washroom. Instead, he figured he'd clean off as much as possible in the trough behind the stable. He took a bar of soap from his saddlebags, two more rags, and headed outside.

Once he reached the trough, Nate removed his hat and bandanna, unbuckled his gunbelt and set it aside, then peeled off his mud-caked shirt. For just a brief moment, he thought about taking off his mud-caked denims and drawers, but quickly discarded that idea. All that would have to happen would be for one of the women on the Circle Dot E to happen by while he was standing there in his birthday suit. That would be embarrassing, to say the least…not to mention it would land him in hot water with Captain Quincy, and the Hennesseys. No, he'd have to wait until he was safely inside the bunkhouse to pull off his pants.

Nate ducked his head in the trough, to soak his hair and wet his face and neck. He took the soap, lathered up, and scrubbed himself off. The trough was in the shade most of the day, so the water it contained was still relatively cool. It was refreshing on Nate's skin on this sweltering day.

Some of the soap got into Nate's eyes, causing them to burn. He ducked his face in the trough once again, trying to stop the stinging. When he straightened back up, he felt two arms wrap around him, and two hands placed on his chest. A pair of soft lips nuzzled his neck.

"Guess who?" a voice whispered.

"*Clarissa?*" Nate exclaimed, not quite believing his ears.

"That's right." Clarissa turned him to face her. "I've been waiting to get you alone for a long, long time."

"But, but you can't," Nate sputtered. "This isn't right. You're Hoot's girl."

"Henry doesn't have any claim on me," Clarissa answered. "I'm no one man's girl." She lifted her face to his. "And right now, at this moment, I'm *your* girl."

"But, Clarissa, I can't do this to my best friend."

"He doesn't ever need to know, unless you tell him."

She kissed Nate full on the lips.

"Nate!" Hoot came out of the stable, then stopped short. He dropped the shovel he was holding and charged his friend. "Just what are you doin'?"

"Hoot, it wasn't me—" Nate's protest was cut off when Hoot lowered his shoulder and rammed it into the pit of Nate's stomach, slamming him back against the stable wall and driving most of the air from his lungs.

"Henry, stop it!" Clarissa cried, to no avail. Stunned, Nate hung against the wall, helpless as Hoot shot three quick punches to his gut; then, as Nate jackknifed, hit him as hard as he could, squarely on the point of his chin. The blow straightened Nate and bounced the back of his head against the wall. Nate sagged to the ground, curled up on his side and holding his middle. Hoot picked up the shovel he'd dropped and swung it over his head, ready to bring it down on the back of Nate's head and smash in his skull.

"Henry, I said stop it," Clarissa repeated, grabbing him by the arm before the blow could be delivered. "I think you've done enough. Let's go. Now. I mean it."

"All right," Hoot said. "But he had no right to be kissin' on you." To Nate, he snarled, "If I ever see you anywhere near Clarissa again I'll finish what I started here. I mean it, Nate. You just stay away from her. And steer clear of me, too. You think you'd be satisfied with that Mexican hot tamale you've been kissin' on, but no, you had to go and try'n steal my gal, too. C'mon Clarissa, let's get outta here."

Taking Clarissa by the arm, Hoot turned and stalked away, leaving Nate lying there, barely conscious. Nate attempted to push himself up, but fell back and lay there, groaning, with blood dripping from his chin, a lump rising on his jaw, and feeling like his belly'd been trampled by a herd of wild horses.

◆●◆

Nate stumbled into the Rangers' bunkhouse shortly before suppertime. His hat was askew, he had his shirt and bandanna draped over one shoulder and his gunbelt over the other. He staggered a bit as he walked toward his bunk.

"Nate, what the heck happened?" Jeb exclaimed. "George said you'd gotten yourself into a fight with a mud puddle, and the puddle won. He sure never said you'd gotten the stuffin's beaten out of you. Who did that to you?"

"I was cleanin' the muck off Red, and he got mad. He pinned me against the back of his stall," Nate answered.

"Red did that to you? I can't hardly believe it," Dan said. "That horse loves you, and trusts you. He'd have no call to do that. Besides, those scrapes and bruises don't look like they came from any horse's hoof, or from being banged against a wall. They look like they came from a fist. Why don't you level with Jeb?"

"Keep outta this, Dan. I told y'all exactly what happened," Nate insisted. He tossed his shirt and bandanna on the floor, and threw his gunbelt on his bunk. "I was combin' the mud outta Red's tail. I must've pulled it too hard, and that hurt him, so he fought back. That's all. Now, just leave me alone, all of you. I want to get out of the rest of these dirty clothes, wash up, and get to bed."

"Not quite so fast there, kid," Jeb answered. "You'd better let me tend to your hurts. They look pretty bad. Hoot, you mind givin' me a hand fixin' up your buddy?"

"Sorry, Jeb." Hoot shook his head from where he was lying on his bunk. "I'm plumb tuckered out, and my back's hurtin' from shovelin' manure out of the stalls most of the afternoon. Besides, you don't need my help tendin' to a few cuts."

Jeb looked from Hoot, to Nate, and back again. Both had their jaws set stubbornly, neither looking at the other.

"All right, Hoot," he said, with a shrug. "Joe, would you mind if I ask you to help out?"

Joe was at one of the tables, playing a game of solitaire. He threw down the jack of diamonds he held, pushed back his chair, and stood up.

"Not at all, Jeb," he said. He shot Hoot a hard look. "That's what pards are for, to look out for each other. That's the only way we can survive out here, watchin' each others' backs. I'll help patch Nate up."

"Thanks, Joe. Go to the cook shack and get some hot water from George," Jeb said. "He's got the bandages and salve in there, too. Nate, you come with me."

"You don't need to be makin' such a fuss over a couple of little bumps," Nate protested.

"Nate, you heard me," Jeb snapped. "Now, either you walk into the wash room on your own two feet, or I'll drag you in there, if I have to. Which is it gonna be?"

"All right." Nate gave in. "I'll go, but I still say you're makin' a big deal out of nothin'."

He headed for the wash room, with Jeb holding his arm to steady him. When they passed Hoot's bunk, he turned onto his belly, and buried his face in his pillow. Nate kept his gaze fixed straight ahead.

"Sit down, Nate," Jeb ordered, once they reached the wash room. He took a basin from the washstand. Nate slumped into a chair.

"You might as well pull off those muddy boots while we're waitin' for Joe," Jeb suggested.

"Okay." Nate bent over to pull off the boots. When he did, a wave of dizziness swept through him. He had to swallow hard to keep down the bile rising in his throat. He did manage to get the boots, and his socks, off, then leaned back in the chair, gasping for breath.

87

"I thought you said you weren't hurt bad, son," Jeb said. "Seems to me you're hurtin' a lot more'n you're lettin' on."

"I'm just a bit sore, that's all," Nate insisted. "And hungry. Once I get some food in my belly I'll be fine and dandy."

"You'd better let me be the judge of that," Jeb answered.

Joe came into the washroom, carrying a pitcher of steaming hot water, a tin of salve, and a stack of clean bandages.

"Here you are, Jeb," he said. He handed the pitcher to him. Jeb poured some of the water into the basin, dipped a cloth into it, and used that to wipe the blood from Nate's chin.

"You've got a pretty good cut here, Nate," he said. "I don't think it'll need stitches, but you might end up with a scar. You're gonna have quite the lump on your jaw, too. You might have trouble chewin' for a spell. I'm gonna wash the cut out now."

Jeb dipped the soap in the water, and rubbed it on the cloth to work up a lather. Nate winced when Jeb pressed the cloth against his chin, and the harsh soap stung the open wound.

"I'm sorry, Nate," Jeb said. "I know it stings like the devil, but there's an awful lot of dirt in that cut. I've gotta get as much of it outta there as I can."

He finished washing out the wound, dried it, and coated it with salve.

"There's no way to put a bandage on that, Nate, short of tyin' your mouth shut," he said, with a chuckle. "Now, there's probably some folks who'd be glad to see you gagged, but I'm not one of those. As long as the salve covers that cut, you should be fine."

"Thanks, Jeb," Nate said. "Can I get up now?"

"Not quite yet," Jeb answered. "I need to make certain you don't have any cracked ribs. It looks like your gut took quite a poundin' when—well, when *your horse* lit into you. Your belly's already turnin' several nice shades of black and blue." He looked hard at Nate while he emphasized the words "your horse".

"He's got a nice lump raisin' on the back of his head, too, Jeb," Joe said, from where he stood behind Nate. "It's big as an egg, and I reckon it's gonna get even a bit larger. I'll get some cool water from the springhouse so we can put a compress on it. Be right back."

"All right, Joe."

While Joe went for the water, Jeb poked and prodded Nate's middle, pressing hard on his ribs. Nate winced whenever he hit a particularly sore spot, but, luckily, there was no sharp pain whenever Jeb pushed on a rib.

"It seems you've only got some real bad bruises, Nate," Jeb said. "But you'll need to be careful for a couple of days, just in case I missed somethin'."

"I will be," Nate assured him.

Joe returned, holding a bucket of water, which he handed to Jeb. Jeb took another clean cloth, soaked it, then pressed it against the lump on the back of Nate's head.

"Hold that there for a few minutes, Nate," he ordered.

Nate kept the compress in place for almost ten minutes, until his arm grew tired.

"You can remove that compress now," Jeb told him. When he did, Jeb studied the lump.

"There's a bit of a cut there," he said. "I'm gonna cover it with salve, then wrap a bandage around your head. It'll only have to stay on for a couple of days. I'll change it tomorrow."

"Okay,"

Jeb soon finished treating the last of Nate's injuries.

"I'm about done here," Jeb said. "I reckon you'll want to finish washin' up. Joe'n I'll leave you to that."

"Thanks, Jeb. You too, Joe. I appreciate everythin' you've done."

"It's nothin'," Jeb said.

"I'm still grateful."

"You might want to be more careful around your horse from now on," Joe said.

"My horse? Oh. Yeah, my horse," Nate echoed. "I reckon you're right. I'll remember that."

"Joe, let's go outside for a smoke, while Nate washes up," Jeb said.

"Outside? It's pretty hot out there. Why not just have a smoke right here?" Joe asked.

"I'd like to get some fresh air," Jeb answered, giving Joe a meaningful look.

"Yeah. Now that you mention it, I reckon I could use some fresh air, too," Joe answered. "Let's go."

He and Jeb went outside. They each stood with one foot braced against the bunkhouse wall while they rolled and lit quirlies.

"What do you think really happened to Nate?" Joe asked. "He sure didn't get those hurts from any horse."

"I dunno for certain," Jeb said. He took a drag on his cigarette. "But I'd bet my hat Hoot's involved, somehow. That's why I didn't want to talk inside. It sure ain't like Hoot, not wantin' to help, especially refusin' to help Nate. They've been friends practically since the day Nate and I rode into camp. You hardly ever see 'em apart. Somethin' just doesn't add up."

"Yeah. And did you see how neither of 'em would look at each other?" Joe said. "Didn't say a word to each other, neither. And Hoot's knuckles are all scraped up. Somethin' sure went sour between those two, all right. You reckon we'll ever find out what it is?"

"I'd imagine we will, Joe. In time," Jeb said. "One of 'em is bound to open up. Then we'll find out the truth. I just hope, whatever's stuck in their craws, it blows over. The quicker, the better. They're both good Rangers, and they're even better as pardners. I'd hate to see that busted up, over what's probably some stupid misunderstanding. And two men at odds with each other is never good in an outfit like ours. Not when we have to depend on each other so much. But, there's nothin' we can do about it, at least not right now. Let's go back in and get ready for supper."

They took final drags on their quirlies, tossed the butts into the dirt and ground them out under their boot heels, then headed back inside.

◆●◆

Nate got rid of his mud-caked denims. The thick mud had soaked clean through the pants and stained his drawers, so he removed those too. He washed off the remaining dirt still clinging to him. After drying off, he went back to his bunk carrying his dirty clothes. He removed his spare drawers, shirt, and pants from the peg where they hung, and his extra pair of socks from his saddlebags. He redressed, then stretched out on his bunk. A few minutes later, Captain Quincy returned. He had been up at the main house, visiting with Charlie Hennessey. He spotted the bandage around Nate's head as soon as he stepped into the bunkhouse.

91

"Nate. What happened to you, son?" he asked. "Have a run-in with a renegade you came across?"

"No, nothin' like that, Cap'n." Nate shook his head. "Me'n Red got tangled up in a big mud puddle, then when I was cleanin' him off I must've tugged on his tail too hard, because he pinned me against the wall. He gave me a good kick in my belly, too. But Jeb and Joe patched me up. I'll be all right."

"I see." Quincy rubbed his chin. "Are you certain that's all that happened? Because if it's anythin' more than that, I'll have to write up a report for Austin."

"No, that's all that happened, Cap'n," Nate assured him. "It was my fault, not bein' more careful while I was workin' on Red."

"Then we'll let it drop, for now," Quincy answered. "Hoot, you might want to keep a closer eye on your pardner. Keep him out of trouble."

"Nate's a big boy now. He can take care of himself," Hoot answered.

"None of us are ever too big we can't use help from time to time. Don't forget that, Harrison," Quincy replied, his voice taut.

"Yessir, Cap'n," Hoot said. "I'll try'n remember."

"See that you do," Quincy said. "I hope George has supper just about ready. I'm starved." He sniffed. "Whatever he's got cookin', it sure smells good."

"He said he was gonna make a big batch of chili," Dan said.

"Sure. It's almost ninety degrees, and he makes chili," Quincy said. "When it was freezin' outside, he was servin' cold mutton."

"He claims the chili's so hot it'll make you feel cool after it wears off," Dan answered. "I hear tell that's a Mexican way of thinking. Hot, spicy food helps you cool down. Dunno if that's true or not, but that's what I've heard. I reckon we're about to find out. Here comes George now."

"Supper's ready," the company cook announced, as he emerged from the cook shack. "Come and get it. Couple of you get the coffee and bread on the table."

There was a mini-stampede when the men raced for the cook shack. They took tin plates and filled them with the thick, spicy chili. Hoot took the coffee pot, Joe the bread and butter, and placed them on the table. Soon, the men were gulping down their meal. Instead of sitting next to or across from each other, as they always did, Nate and Hoot sat at opposite ends of the table. The other Rangers exchanged glances when they noticed, but said nothing.

Nate had gotten used to the spicier food served in much of Texas over the past months. However, this chili was extra hot. He felt his face flush, and sweat bead on his forehead, after the first few spoonsful. He noticed the other men all seemed to be having the same reaction. Evidently, George had indeed made this batch extra hot. The crusty bread he'd baked, still warm and slathered with freshly churned butter from the Hennesseys' larder, took away some of its bite. And, as the first effect wore off, it seemed, to Nate at least, he did feel a bit cooler. Everyone went back for seconds, some even for thirds.

"George," Captain Quincy said, once everyone was finished and sitting with last cups of coffee, "I have to say, this was one of the finest meals you've come up with in a long time. It was delicious."

"Why, thank you kindly, Cap'n," George answered.

"It surely was," Jeb added. The other men murmured their assent.

"I appreciate that," George said. "Of course, I can do a

lot more here, where I've got a real stove to work with, than on the trail. But I'm glad you boys enjoyed this supper. Did any of you happen to enjoy it enough to help me clean up?"

"I'll give you a hand," Nate offered.

"I'd be obliged," George said, "But you'd better try'n rest up from those hurts, son."

"He's right, Nate," Jeb agreed. "George, I'll help with the dishes."

"Then, that's settled. Thanks, Jeb."

While George and Jeb cleaned up, the other men drifted back to their bunks, or sat at the table, talking or playing cards. Nate got out his gun cleaning kit to clean and oil his mud-clogged pistol, then, once that was finished and the gun reassembled, crawled into bed. He lay on his back, staring at the ceiling for nearly an hour before sleep finally claimed him.

The next day, after checking on Rig Bed, Nate hung around outside the bunkhouse, sitting in the sun and letting it warm his face. He tried to visit with Consuela, but she was occupied with helping make a dress for Claire. He did have the chance to give her a quick explanation of why he sported a bandage around his head, and had a cut-open chin. She promised to meet him that evening, once her work was done.

Around mid-afternoon, Hoot came outside. He'd spent the day mending his gunbelt. He started to walk past Nate.

"Hoot," Nate called after him. "We've gotta talk."

"We've got nothin' to talk about," Hoot answered.

"I'm sorry, but we sure do," Nate said. "What you saw

yesterday wasn't what you thought it was. I didn't start anythin'. It was Clarissa. I was just tryin' to clean up, when she snuck up behind me and wrapped her arms around me. I had soap in my eyes, and didn't even know she was there. Next thing I know, she's huggin' on me, and tryin' to kiss me."

"That's a dirty lie," Hoot snapped.

"It's the truth," Nate insisted. "I tried to make her stop. Told her she was your girl, but she said she wasn't any man's girl. Said she'd kiss whoever she wanted, whenever she wanted. That's what happened, Hoot. I dunno if you'll believe me or not, but that's exactly what happened."

"Nate, I thought you were a good man, and my best friend," Hoot answered. "Now, instead of owning up to what you pulled, you go'n dirty the name of a fine gal like Clarissa. She told me what really happened, that she was walkin' past, then you grabbed her and forced yourself on her. I ought to gut-shoot you where you stand for that. And if I ever see you near her again, I will."

"She's lyin' to you, Hoot," Nate said. "I can't make you believe that, but she is. I didn't do anythin' to her, in fact, I tried to push her off. But if you don't want to listen, there's nothin' else I can say."

"There sure ain't," Hoot answered. "The only thing you can do is stay away from me."

He stalked off, leaving Nate slumped miserably in his chair.

◆●◆

That evening, as she'd promised, Consuela met Nate. They sat side by side in rockers on the main house's front porch, holding hands while they talked. Nate explained to her the whole sorry incident with Clarissa and Hoot.

95

Consuela sighed before answering.

"I was afraid this would happen," she said. "I had hoped Hoot would not be hurt by Clarissa, but I am not surprised. I wish he had taken up with her sister, Claire. She's a much nicer girl. I hate to use such language, but in my country, Clarissa would be called a *puta*. She is not a good woman for any man, let alone one as fine and honorable as your friend seems to be."

"A *puta*? What's that?" Nate asked.

Consuela thought for a moment.

"How can I put this to you politely, Nate? In terms that a decent woman would use? She's a girl who, shall we say, throws herself at men. She's a *desvergonzada...*a hussy."

"I'd seen her with a couple of the cowboys," Nate said, "but I never really gave it much thought. I figured she was just bein' friendly. And I sure couldn't say anythin' about it to Hoot. He'd never have believed me. Heck, look what he did to me when he found me'n her. I think he'd have killed me if Clarissa hadn't stopped him. I tried to tell him what happened, but he won't listen. I've gotta try'n figure out how to make him realize I'm tellin' the truth."

"If Hoot is that blind about Clarissa, nothing you can say to him will change his mind," Consuela said. "He's going to have to find out for himself. And when he does discover the truth, I'm afraid he's going to be hurt, very badly. Now, enough talk of them. You are here, with me. That's what matters. Let's just enjoy this beautiful evening."

The weather had cooled considerably, with a light breeze out of the north, and a nearly full moon hung in the sky. Consuela leaned her head on Nate's shoulder. He placed an arm around her. He wanted to do more, but his battered ribs refused to allow it. Even the kiss he attempted to sneak was painful, due to the cut on his chin and bruised jaw. He settled for just sitting with her, enjoying her company, and thinking about what the future might bring.

6

The next day, Nate was watching as several cowboys drove in a small herd of horses, which were to be broken for the summer's work. As they drew nearer, he shook his head and smiled. The four men working the herd were the youngest hands on the Circle Dot E. Two of them were the sandy-haired young cowboys, Zack Ellesio and Justin Bendlak. The third was dark-haired Nicolas Pearson, and the fourth was lanky Kyle Newton. They moved the forty or so horses effortlessly, keeping them at a steady trot, easily turning back any stragglers. It didn't take long before they had run the entire herd into a corral and shut them in.

Kids sure grow up a lot faster out here than back home, Nate thought, as he watched the boys dismount. All four were in full cowboy gear, including six guns at their hips, and Kyle had a huge chaw of tobacco bulging out his cheek. In Wilmington, boys this age would generally be in school; or, on days classes were out, playing with their friends or just lazing around. Of course, some of his friends did help out in their parents' stores, but those were the exception. True, there were those kids, from poorer families, who had to work long hours in some of the factories, hustle newspapers, shine shoes, or find some other means of bringing in cash to help put food on the table, but not in Nate's comfortable former world.

Here, in Texas, things were different. Almost every boy over ten or twelve seemed to have a job of some kind, mostly as ranch hands. Heck, he'd even seen girls, including the Hennessey daughters, help drive cattle, or doctor an injured calf. Life was hard on the frontier, and it took every member of a family, working together, to survive.

Nate glanced up at a smudge of dust which appeared on the horizon. The dust soon materialized into a group of oncoming horsemen. When they drew nearer, he recognized them as another of the patrols Captain Quincy had sent out, now returning. This one was led by Lieutenant Bob Berkeley. Riding with him were the company's Tonkawa scout, Percy Leaping Buck, Diego Sandoval, Tom Tomlinson, and Morey Carson. Nate walked over to meet them as they rode up to the barn and dismounted.

"Take care of your horses, men, then we'll see if George has anythin' keepin' warm on the stove," Berkeley ordered. "Howdy, Nate. Things quiet around here?"

"Howdy, Bob," Nate said. "Yeah, I'd say they are. Cap'n Quincy's just waitin' for all the boys to ride in, and on word from Austin as to where we're headed next."

"Well, that might be about to change," Berkeley said. "Do me a favor, Nate. Let Dave know I need to speak with him, as soon as I get my horse settled. Also, tell him I'd like any of the other men who are around to be there, too."

"Sure. Be glad to," Nate answered.

"Much obliged," Berkeley said. "Tell him I'll be with him in about half an hour."

"All right, Bob."

Nate walked up to the bunkhouse. He found Captain Quincy in his office, working on reports. The captain looked up when Nate knocked at his door.

"Nate. C'mon in," he said. "Anythin' I can do for you?"

"Yeah, Cap'n. Lieutenant Bob and his men just rode in," Nate said. "The lieutenant says he has somethin' important to tell you. Says he'll be here in here in half an hour, once he takes care of his horse. He wants all the men here."

"Okay, Nate. Thanks for lettin' me know. Bob didn't give you any idea what he wanted to talk about?"

"No, sir, Cap'n Dave, he didn't. Just said he needed to speak with you."

"All right, Nate. We'll just have to wait to see what he has to say. Gather all the others, will you?"

"Sure, Cap'n. See you in a bit."

Most of the men were resting in the bunkhouse. Nate told those there would be a meeting shortly, then went to find the others. Jeb and Dan were at the smithy, re-shoeing their horses. Nate sent them to the bunkhouse, then set out to find Hoot. He located him at the main house, sitting on a bench in the back yard, with Clarissa at his side. She blushed slightly at Nate's approach.

"Get outta here, Nate," Hoot snapped, the minute he saw him. "I warned you to stay away from me, and especially Clarissa."

"Sorry, Hoot. I don't mean to bother you, but this can't be helped. Lieutenant Bob's patrol just came in."

"Yeah, I saw 'em," Hoot said. "What's that got to do with you comin' up here?"

"Bob's asked Cap'n Dave to have a meetin' with all of us. It's in about twenty minutes from now. I just came to let you know."

"Well, you have, so get outta here," Hoot said. "Tell Cap'n Dave I'll be right along."

"Okay, Hoot. Hoot—"

"What?"

"Oh, never mind."

◆●◆

Thirty minutes later, the Rangers were gathered in the bunkhouse. Captain Quincy called for quiet.

"Men, Lieutenant Berkeley's got somethin' he needs to share with us, so listen up."

The room fell silent.

"Thanks, boys. I'm gonna make this short and sweet," Berkeley began. "We've been patrollin' a bit south of here, along the Rio. We didn't have much luck, but did find out somethin' that's gonna mean real trouble. Black Dog and his bunch are back in Texas, raidin' all up and down the river. We got word they're headin' this way. For you new men, Black Dog's a Comanche who jumped the reservation, up in the Territories, a couple of years back, with about thirty other braves. He made his way into Mexico, and has been raisin' all sorts of Cain down there. Evidently, he's decided to see if the pickin's on this side of the border are easier. He's hit three ranches already. This one could well be next."

"We think he'll strike sometime within the next three days," Percy continued. "Because he hasn't been challenged since he came back into Texas, he's gotten bolder. Each place he's hit has been bigger than the last."

"How about sendin' some men out after him?" Joe asked.

Berkeley shook his head. "It wouldn't work. Black Dog would just fade away into the hills. We've been lookin' for sign of him. As you all know, Percy's one of the best trackers in the Rangers, and even he lost Black Dog's trail.

And Diego grew up in these parts. He knows this territory as well as any man, better'n most, and he couldn't find any sign of Black Dog, either. Since there's no other spreads between the Cross M, where he struck last, and here, we figure the Circle Dot E's his next target. We'll just have to let him ride on in, and be ready for him when he comes. That means men on guard, day and night. We'll put our horses inside the stable. We can't chance havin' those Comanch' runnin' 'em off, leavin' us no way to pursue 'em, if they make good on their raid."

"I thought Indians didn't attack at night," Nate said. "Only in the daytime."

"Nate, get that darn fool notion about Indians attacking only at night out of your head right now, or you're liable to catch a Comanche or Apache arrow in your gut," Jeb retorted. "Some Indians might prefer to fight only durin' the day, but most of 'em'll attack whenever it suits their fancy."

"Jeb's right, Nate," Percy said. "And there's gonna be a full Comanche moon tomorrow night. From what I know of Black Hawk, he'll make his move then. Another reason I'm positive he'll hit this ranch is that herd of horses in the corral. It's a mighty tempting prize for any Comanche. If Black Dog can steal those horses, it'll be a real honor for him. His status as a warrior will rise considerably."

"Which means all of you pull double duty tomorrow," Captain Quincy said. "Bob, Percy, come with me, and we'll get things set. The rest of you, wait here, until you get your assignments."

The captain, Berkeley, and Percy went back to his office. The other men discussed the new revelation while they waited.

"Jeb, what's a Comanche moon?" Nate asked.

"It's a full moon, most usually called that durin' the spring and summer," Jeb explained. "The Comanch' like to raid under a 'Comanche' moon, since it's so bright. Like Percy said, I'd bet my life Black Dog will hit us sometime in the next two nights."

"Your life is exactly what you'll be bettin', if Black Dog hits us at full strength," Diego said. "He's cunning, smart, tough, and vicious. It'll take everythin' we've got to beat him. And a lot of luck besides." He crossed himself.

◆●◆

Every man on the Circle Dot E was posted on sentry duty the next night. Some were several hundred yards from the buildings, wherever there was enough cover to conceal them. The rest were stationed around the houses, stables, and outbuildings. Nate was posted behind the main stable, along with Morey Carson and Tom Tomlinson. With them were several men from the ranch: Hunt Knudsen, the head wrangler, Harry Cole, a veteran cowboy, and two of the younger cowboys, Zack Ellesio and Justin Bendlak. When it came to an Indian or outlaw attack, it didn't matter how young or old a man was. He had to help defend himself and his comrades. It didn't much matter to renegades how old a man was, anyway. They'd kill an eight-year-old as readily as a full-grown man, without a second thought. In the main house, some of the women were prepared to pass out ammunition and reload rifles for the fighters. Others were in the kitchen, ready to tend to any of the wounded.

"Tom, you've fought Indians before, haven't you?" Nate asked.

"I reckon a time or two," Tom answered. "Why?"

"I'm just wonderin'. What time do you think they'll hit

us?"

"With Indians, you never know. A lotta times they'll strike at dawn, when folks are tired from watchin' for 'em all night. But to others, it don't really matter. We'll just have to stay sharp. Boy howdy, I could sure use a smoke."

Captain Quincy had ordered no smoking, lest the glow of a cigarette or the whiff of tobacco smoke give away a man's position.

"I can't offer you a smoke, but you can take a swallow of my whiskey," Morey offered, pulling a flask from his shirt pocket and holding it out.

"Not right now, Morey, thanks," Tom said.

"Well, don't mind if I do," Morey said. He uncorked the flask and took a good-sized gulp.

"You should probably lay off that stuff for a bit, Morey," Tom cautioned. "You seem to hit it pretty heavy."

"It helps me keep my wits about me," Morey answered. He took another drink.

"Nate, when I found you down by the Rio, I sure as heck never figured I'd be fightin' alongside you," Zack said. "I'm real glad you Rangers are here."

"Yeah," Justin added. "We'd have been overrun and all of us killed for certain if you weren't. There's not a chance we could've held off a bunch like Black Dog's without help."

"Your guns are gonna come in handy, too," Nate said.

"You boys might want to quiet down, so we can hear them Comanch' when they do come in," Hunt said.

"Hunt's right, boys," Cole agreed. "They're just as likely to sneak up on us, real quiet-like, rather'n ridin' in whoopin' and hollerin' like the Devil."

The men waited for the attack until well into the early hours of the morning. Despite their anxiety, their eyelids grew heavy as sleep tried to claim them. After long hours of gazing into the night, wondering if every movement in the shadows was a Comanche warrior sneaking up on them, weariness was taking its toll. Several times, Nate found himself nodding off. He had just shaken himself awake once again when the night was pierced by a screech of terror, followed by the crackling of rifle fire and the hoof beats of fast-ridden horses. Hard on those came the war whoops of Black Dog and his Comanches.

"Here they come. Up and at 'em, boys!" Tom shouted, as the Indians crested the rise. "Make every shot count."

He waited until the marauders drew closer, leveled his rifle, and shot. An Indian pony went down, his rider rolling off, hitting the ground, and springing to his feet. Tom shot him through the chest. This time, the Indian went down for keeps.

Within minutes, Black Dog's warriors seemed to be everywhere. Bullets sought out their victims, arrows flew through the night, to bury themselves in their targets. Nate aimed and fired as fast as he could, only pausing to reload. His Winchester's barrel grew hot. Around him, the other men were also fighting a pitched battle. Without warning, Nate heard a sound he would never forget, the sound of an arrow thudding into human flesh. Morey Carson fell back, dead, with that arrow in his chest.

Kyle Newton came running from the corner of the barn. "There's too many of 'em," he shouted.

"Get down, kid!" Hunt yelled, too late. An arrow buried itself in the lanky young cowboy's belly. Kyle grunted, doubled over, dropped to his knees, then pitched to his face. Zack took careful aim at the warrior who had gotten Kyle. He pulled the trigger, and the Comanche went down, with a bullet in his stomach.

"Got that one, anyway," Zack muttered. "Kyle, that's for you, pardner." Alongside him, Justin also took a shot at a warrior on horseback, riding straight at them. His bullet somersaulted the brave off his horse, to lie motionless in the dirt.

"I got one too, Zack!" he shouted. "Hit him dead center." He aimed and fired again. His shot took a Comanche in his side. The Indian slumped over his horse's neck, hung on for a few strides, then lost his grip and slid to the ground.

From above, there came a screech of pain, when Tom Clancy, the cowboy assigned to the hayloft, took a bullet in his gut. He doubled over, fell from the loft, and landed at Justin's feet.

"They...they got Tom," he stammered, staring at the dead cowboy.

"Just keep on fightin', or they'll get all of *us*, dead center," Tom said. "And I'm kinda fond of my scalp. I don't cotton to the notion of it hangin' from a Comanche's coup stick."

"I don't imagine any of us hanker for that," Hunt said.

Tom took another shot, cursing when it missed his target. The Indians were more wary now, not moving in quite so closely, choosing their targets more carefully. Zack grunted when an arrow sliced along his ribs.

"You all right, Zack?" Nate asked.

"I...I think so," Zack answered. "It feels like it's just a deep cut. It hurts like blazes, though." He took another shot, and yet one more Indian rode out of the fight, slumped over his horse's neck, with Zack's bullet in his shoulder.

All around the Circle Dot E, desperate battles were taking place. Men on both sides went down, with bullets or arrows in them. The Comanches concentrated their attack on the ranch house and the main stable, hoping to drive off the horses there. A flaming arrow embedded itself in the house's roof, instantly igniting the tinder-dry cedar shakes. Brian Hennessey was stationed on the roof for just such an eventuality. He dropped his rifle, grabbed the wet blanket alongside him, and rushed to smother the flames. He had no sooner gotten them extinguished when a bullet took him in the back. Brian arched in pain, fell, and rolled off the roof, to land face down in the dirt. A Comanche leapt from his horse, brandishing a skinning knife. He grabbed Brian's hair, intending to take his scalp. A bullet from the house cut him down. He crumpled, falling across Brian's lifeless body.

As suddenly as they had appeared, the Indians retreated, whooping and hollering in triumph. They had overrun the men defending the horse corral, chased out the horses, and were driving the stolen animals in front of them as they disappeared into the night, hurried along by bullets from the Rangers and ranch hands.

"You reckon they'll be back, Tom?" Nate asked.

"I doubt it," Tom answered. "They got what they wanted, a whole bunch of horses. But I'll guarantee you one thing. They ain't seen the last of us. Cap'n Quincy'll have us ridin' after 'em come first light. For now, it's time to count our losses and lick our wounds. How you doin', Zack?"

"I'll be okay," Zack assured him. He pulled off his bandanna, folded it, and stuffed it inside his shirt to slow the blow of blood. "Just need to get myself patched up, and I'll be good as new."

"How about you, Justin?"

The young cowboy had a bloody gash just above his left

ear, where a bullet had torn off a piece of flesh, as well as a good-sized chunk of his hair.

"I should be all right, too," Justin answered. "I'll bet I've got a heck of a headache come mornin', though."

"I wouldn't take that bet," Tom answered. "I reckon we'd better get you both up to the house, and get you taken care of. There's nothin' we can do for Morey."

"Nothin' we can do for Harry, either," Hunt said. "They got him, too. Guess we'll have some buryin's come mornin'."

The veteran cowboy had fallen with an arrow through his throat.

◆●◆

Captain Quincy had taken charge of the rescue efforts, once the Comanches had gone. Nine Circle Dot E men, including Brian Hennessey, were dead, with several more wounded. Among the Rangers, besides Morey Carson, Dan Morton and Joe Duffy had also been killed. Their throats had been slit by Comanches who had slipped up on them, while they were guarding the perimeter of the ranch. Captain Quincy had a bloody left arm, and Diego Sandoval a bullet hole through his thigh.

"How bad we'd get hit, Cap'n?" Tom asked, once he and his partners reached the house. "We lost Morey, and two of the ranch hands."

"That's three more men we lost. They hit us bad enough," Quincy answered. "But at least they didn't get our horses, just that herd the boys drove in. We'll be headin' out after 'em soon as we bury our dead and tend to the wounded. That'll be at false dawn. And we gave better'n we got. We killed at least a dozen Comanch'."

"As many of my men as you need will ride with you,"

Charlie Hennessey said.

"I appreciate the offer. We'll see, once we've figured out for certain how bad off y'all are here," Quincy said.

Louella Hennessey came onto the porch. Her eyes were red from weeping over her dead son, Brian. However, like most ranch wives, she was a brave woman, tough enough to handle the hardships and dangers of the Texas frontier. Despite her loss, she would maintain her composure.

"Captain Quincy, bring your men inside," she said. "We'll treat your injured. There's coffee ready for all of you."

"Much obliged," Quincy answered. "C'mon, men, you heard the lady."

Claire Hennessey came outside, to stand alongside her mother.

"Mother," she said. "Have you seen Josiah?"

"No, why?" Louella answered. "Wasn't he with you?"

"Not since just after the Indians attacked," Claire said.

"The last I saw of him he was headed for the stable," Nicolas Pearson said, from where he stood on the porch. "He said he wanted to make certain no Comanch' got his pet pony. I tried to stop him, but he pulled away from me."

"Josiah! Charlie, those Indians have Josiah!" Louella cried.

"Just take it easy. We don't know that yet for certain," Hennessey answered. "We'll take a look around. I'm sure he's hunkered down somewhere, hidin' until he knows it's safe. He'll turn up."

"We'll give you a hand lookin' for the boy," Quincy offered. "Don't worry, Mrs. Hennessey. We'll find him."

Every man still able to walk fanned out to look for the missing boy. However, their search was futile. There was no sign of Josiah anywhere. His wiry pinto was also

109

missing. Mrs. Hennessey was waiting anxiously on the porch when the last man, Hoot Harrison, returned.

"You didn't have any luck either, Hoot?" Quincy asked him.

"No sir, Cap'n Dave. I'd say the boy's gone," Hoot answered.

"That means the Comanches must have him," Louella said. "Captain, you have to go after them, right now. I've already lost one son tonight. I couldn't stand it if I also lost another."

Captain Quincy shook his head.

"I'm sorry, Mrs. Hennessey. We'd never be able to trail those Comanch' in the dark, even with the full moon. Plus, it'd be too easy for 'em to ambush us at night."

"But they have Josiah!"

"I know that," Quincy answered softly, trying to reassure the frantic mother. "We'll bury our deed, have breakfast, then start after 'em, soon as it's light enough to see. Percy, my scout, is one of the best trackers I've ever worked with. We'll find your boy, and bring him back. I promise you that."

"But what if they get into Mexico before you catch up with 'em, Ranger?" Hennessey asked. "You're not allowed to cross the Rio. If they make it across, we'll never see Josiah again."

"What Rio?" Quincy answered.

7

As did most isolated ranches in the West, where death was all too common, the Circle Dot E had its own cemetery in a far corner of the spread. With it being essential to get on the trail of Black Dog and his warriors before they could make good their escape, Captain Quincy and the Rangers would not be able to stay for the burial of the dead. Once the wounded had been cared for, the men killed in Black Dog's raid were wrapped in blankets and laid out on the porch. A few prayers were said over them by Captain Quincy and Mr. Hennessey. It would fall to the men remaining behind to load the bodies in a buckboard, dig their graves, and bury them. Once the brief service was over preparations were made to pursue the Comanches. Horses were grained, their shoes checked, then saddled and bridled. Food was prepared, since there would be no breakfast, but only what would be gulped down as the men rode.

Reluctantly, Captain Quincy had to leave Diego behind, due to his wounded leg. Diego knew the territory better than anyone, but his wound would not allow him to do the hard riding required in this pursuit. The Rangers would have to rely on Percy Leaping Buck's considerable skills as a tracker to locate their quarry. The captain had also wanted to leave Nate behind, but Nate convinced him his bruises were not serious enough to keep him out of the saddle.

Charlie Hennessey had demanded he, and as many of his men he could spare from the ranch, accompany the Rangers. His son Luke had also insisted to go along. His father finally convinced him he was needed at home, to stay with his mother and sisters, while his brother Brian was laid to rest. In addition, a contingent of fighters would need to remain behind, in case of another attack on the ranch. Luke would be in charge of those.

The gray light of the false dawn was a streak on the eastern horizon, the men saddling their horses, when Jim Kelly, Ken Demarest, Carl Swan, and Shad Bruneau rode into the yard.

"Cap'n," Jim called to Quincy. "We were patrollin' a bit north of here when we got word Black Dog was on the loose. We rode all night to try'n warn you." He looked at the blanket wrapped bodies lying on the porch. "I guess we were a bit too late."

"You were, Jim," Quincy said. "He hit us hard last night. Killed several men—includin' three of ours—Dan, Joe, and Morey. He also took Josiah Hennessey. We're goin' after him. Rope out some fresh horses, if you think you're not too worn out to ride with us. We're pullin' out in five minutes."

"Of course we're ridin' with you," Jim answered. "C'mon, men, let's get those mounts."

While they waited for Jim and the others to get new horses and transfer their gear onto them, the men finished tacking up. Most of them lit the last cigarettes they would be allowed, until they caught up with Black Dog. Nate was stroking Big Red's neck when Consuela came up to him. She had a sack in one hand, and a brightly colored, striped silk scarf in the other.

"Nate, I packed some extra bacon and *tortillas* for you," she said.

"Why, *gracias,* Consuela. You didn't have to go to all that bother," Nate answered.

"It was no bother at all. I also have this scarf for you, to bring you luck, to remind you of me, and that I want you to come back to me, safely."

She pressed the scarf into Nate's hand. He took it and tied it around his neck, over the bandanna he already wore.

"I'm not gonna take this off until I see you again," he promised her.

"Time to mount up and ride out," Captain Quincy called. Jim and his men had returned, already sitting their horses.

"Be careful, Nate," Consuela pleaded. She gave him a kiss on the cheek.

"I will be," Nate promised, as he swung onto Red's back. *"Hasta luego."*

"Vaya con Dios."

"Men, move out!" Captain Quincy waved the column of riders into motion. Nate suddenly realized Clarissa Hennessey was nowhere in sight. He had only a moment to wonder why, before Quincy increased the horses' gait into a trot.

◆●◆

Captain Quincy and Lieutenant Berkeley rode at the head of the column, with Jeb right behind them. Alongside him was Jim Kelly. Hoot and Nate weren't in their usual spots, at the rear of the company, riding side by side, laughing and joking. This time, Hoot was riding alongside

Carl Swan. Nate and Tom Tomlinson brought up the rear.

"You're not ridin' with Nate, Hoot?" Ken asked.

"Nope."

"You mind tellin' me why?"

"Let's just say he's not the friend I thought he was, and let it go at that," Hoot said.

"All right." Ken gave a shrug. "I won't put my nose where it's not wanted."

The sun burst over the horizon in glorious shades of orange, gold, and crimson. Percy rode up to Captain Quincy.

"I'm gonna ride ahead a bit, and see if I can get a feel for which way Black Dog's headed," he said. "Not that it appears it's gonna be too hard to trail him. These tracks he's leavin' are pretty plain. It's hard to hide the hoof prints of a whole horse herd. Besides, it doesn't appear he's in all that much of a hurry. I think he believes he killed just about everyone back on the Circle Dot E. I'd guess he has no idea anyone'd be on his trail this quick."

"All right, Percy," Quincy said. Percy put his pinto into a lope, and was soon out of sight.

"I sure hope Percy's right, and we catch up with that devil and his bunch before too long," Bob said. "They can make the Rio and be across in a couple of hours, if they've a mind to."

"There's also a thousand or more canyons, arroyos, and draws they can just fade away into, and disappear," Jeb added. "Let's hope Black Dog doesn't do that. He can ambush us real easy, if he does."

"We should find Black Dog before too long," Quincy answered. "He and his braves can't travel as fast as we can, not pushin' those stolen horses. Findin' him shouldn't be the problem. Takin' care of his bunch, once

114

and for all, and gettin' young Josiah Hennessey back, alive, is the real headache we're facing."

Jeb glanced back to where Charlie Hennessey was leading his men, behind the Rangers.

"You reckon Hennessey realizes his boy might already be dead, Dave?" he asked. "Or that he might be killed once Black Dog figures out we're after him?"

"I'm sure it's crossed his mind," Quincy answered. "But I doubt Black Dog has killed the boy, at least not yet. He might, if Josiah causes too much trouble, or slows those Comanch' down too much. But my guess is he wants to take Josiah back to his woman. He'll either turn the boy into a slave, or raise him like his own son, as a Comanche. At any rate, their trail is still pretty clear, and we could be runnin' short of time. Let's pick up the pace."

He put his horse into a ground-eating lope, the rest of the men strung out behind.

◆●◆

An hour later, a rider appeared in the distance, heading toward the Rangers at a full gallop.

"That's Percy, ridin' hard for us," Bob said. "You reckon he's got some of Black Dog's men on his tail?"

"I doubt it," Quincy answered. "I don't see any dust on his trail. My guess is he's caught sight of Black Dog." He held up a hand, ordering the men to a halt. A moment later, Percy rode up to them. He pulled his lathered horse to a sliding stop.

"What've you got, Percy?" Quincy asked.

"Black Dog's about two miles ahead of us, just short of the Rio," the Tonkawa scout answered. "He's got Josiah, as we figured. Looks like he's plannin' to ford the river and cross into Mexico. If we hurry, we can catch him right in the middle of the river. It'd be the best place to hit him. There's lots of scrub and cover on either bank, so it'd be hard to chouse him outta that brush. If we attack while his bunch is still crossin', we'll catch him in the open."

"Good work, Percy," Quincy answered. "Is there any way we can split up, and come at him from two sides?"

"Not until we're almost on top of him; and by that time, Black Dog will have spotted us," Percy answered. "The best way to attack is spread out as soon as we reach the Rio. With luck, we'll get to Black Dog just before he starts to cross. If we do, we'll be able to drive him and his braves right into the water. The river's runnin' pretty high, so they'll have to try'n swim their horses to escape. I'd say we've got a good chance of riddin' ourselves of Black Dog for good."

"Then that's how we'll handle it," Quincy agreed. "Jeb, you and Percy ride back, and let the men know our plan. Remind Hennessey he and his men are to strictly follow my orders. Make certain of that. He'll have only one thing on his mind, rescuin' his boy, and probably won't be thinkin' straight. We can't have him goin' off half-cocked. If he does, that might well spook Black Dog. If that happens, we'll never see him, or Hennessey's boy, again. Have everyone check their weapons."

"Right, Cap'n."

Quincy waited while Jeb and Percy rode among the men, explaining his and Captain Quincy's plan of action. Some of the men murmured a question, others nodded silent understanding.

"Tom," Nate said, while they were still waiting to move out, "It seems a real shame, havin' to fight Indians all the time like this. It seems to me there's plenty of land out here for everybody. Doesn't seem right that the

Comanches and Kiowas keep on killin' white folks. And that we keep killin' them."

"It is a shame," Tom agreed. "It wasn't always this way. Sam Houston, the hero of the Texas Revolution and Texas's first president, when she was still her own country, wanted the whites and Indians to live together in peace. There were quite a few friendly tribes living in Texas back in those days. There were the Tonkawas, like Percy, of course. Then there were Cherokees and Choctaws, who were driven from their homelands back East, and settled in Texas. It seemed things between the Indians and white man would settle down, once some of the warrior societies, like the Karankawas, Comanches, and Apaches were tamed."

"What happened to change that?"

"Mirabeau Lamar, Texas's third president, is what happened. He hated all Indians, and was determined to annihilate every last one of 'em, or drive 'em all out of the country. Lots of folks think of him as a hero, but Sam Houston sure didn't. He hated the man, with good reason. From what I know of Lamar, he was one prejudiced, nasty, hateful individual."

"So just one man caused most of the trouble in Texas between the Indians and the whites?"

"One man, and a lot who agreed with him," Tom said. "And plenty of folks still do. Of course, you can't lay all the blame on the white man. Tribes like the Comanches, Kiowas, and Apaches are warrior societies. To them, it's a great honor to raid, loot, and kill as much as you can. It's their way of life. Most of 'em don't want to change their ways, so they fight, rather'n bein' forced off land that's always been theirs, at least in their minds, and be pushed onto reservations. It don't matter to them that they took a lot of the land they claim as their ancestral home from other tribes, like the Tonkawas. And as you already know, a lot of people think all Indians are savages, no matter what tribe they come from, because some, like the Comanches and Apaches, take scalps and such. Let me tell you, Nate, I've seen atrocities committed by whites or Mexicans that were just as bad, or worse, than any done by an Indian. No, I'd say there's plenty of blame to go around on all sides. And I don't see any end to the fightin' and killin'. Not in our lifetimes, anyway."

"Rangers, ho!"

"Time to move out," Tom said. "And add our own chapter to this sad history."

◆●◆

The Rangers and Circle Dot E men rode at a full gallop the rest of the distance to the Rio Grande. As Percy had hoped, Black Dog and his warriors were gathered on the riverbank, just starting to push the stolen horses into the fast running river. Surrounded by the Comanches was Josiah Hennessey, tied hand and foot to the saddle on his pet pinto.

"Spread out, and fire when ready," Quincy shouted, as the men topped the bank, and rode hell bent for leather down the steep slope, directly at the bunched Indians. Startled by the completely unexpected appearance of the Rangers, the Comanches broke into war cries, and grabbed for their weapons.

A volley of rifle fire came from the Rangers' guns, and several Comanches were shot out of their saddles.

"Make your shots count!" Quincy yelled. "And careful of the boy! Carl, you watch where you point that scattergun of yours."

Carl had already fired both barrels of his shotgun, the bunched shot raking the Comanches.

The Comanches were now beginning to return fire, but the sight of the Rangers bearing down on them caused them to shoot too hastily. Only one bullet found its mark, one that hit Shad in the shoulder, and knocked him out of his saddle. Caught between the hard charging lawmen and the milling, panicked horses, the Indians had no way to escape. Three more went down, with bullets in them, then the rest turned their horses and forced them into the river. Black Dog was in the lead, pulling along Josiah's horse. The Rangers and their partners splashed into the water, hard on their heels.

Hoot had reached midstream, where the water ran deep and fast. He took a bead on an Indian's back, but before he could shoot, an arrow took him high on the left side of his chest and knocked him off his horse. The swift current caught him and swept him downstream.

"Help!" he cried. "I can't swim...not...not...that good—" His words were cut off when the river pulled him under. He surfaced, struggling, twenty feet downstream.

"Hoot! Hang on!" Nate shouted. "C'mon, Red, let's get him." He ripped the big sorrel around and sent him plunging into the river. The horse swam powerfully, and pushed along by the current, was soon overtaking Hoot.

"Gimme your hand, Hoot!" Nate ordered, leaning far over in the saddle. "We've only got one chance." He wrapped his right hand in Red's thick mane, and reached out with his left to grab Hoot's outstretched hand. Hoot's waterlogged clothes and boots dragged him down. For a tense moment, it appeared Nate would lose his grip, but finally, he pulled Hoot alongside his horse.

"Hang onto my saddle, and I'll try'n make shore," Nate

ordered. He turned Red toward the Texas riverbank. Fighting the current, the horse swam until his hooves struck the gravelly river bottom. He lunged out of the water, and onto a spit of sand. Nate let go of Hoot's hand, then jumped from his saddle. Hoot was struggling to breathe. Nate pounded him on the back. Hoot choked, then expelled a good amount of water from his lungs.

"Nate," he gasped, his voice hoarse.

"Shh. Don't say anythin', Hoot'," Nate advised. "Just try'n catch your breath."

◆●◆

Back upstream, the Rangers' attack on Black Dog's Comanches had turned into a complete rout. Nicolas Pearson, one of the Circle Dot E hands, shot a brave riding behind Black Dog. The Comanche fell from his horse, giving Jeb a clear shot at Black Dog, who had dropped the reins of Josiah's horse and was whipping his pony, urging it into deeper water. Jeb pulled Dudley to a halt, took careful aim at the back of the Comanche chief's head, and pulled the trigger. His bullet buried itself deep in Black Dog's brain. He toppled into the river, his body disappearing under the murky water.

Now free, Josiah attempted to turn his horse, but was hampered by his bound hands. He was unable to maneuver the horse, who stumbled into deeper water. The small pinto floundered in the swift current. Nicolas dug his spurs into his chestnut's ribs, sending the gelding leaping ahead.

"I've got you, Josiah," he shouted, as he grabbed the pinto's trailing reins. "You're all right now."

He led the horse back to the riverbank. Charlie Hennessey jumped from his horse, ran up to Josiah, pulled out his knife, slashed the rawhide ropes binding his son, and lifted him from the saddle. He hugged him tightly.

"Josiah, don't you ever do anythin' so dang foolish like this again, tryin' to take on a whole bunch of renegade Indians," he scolded. "You scared me and your ma half to death. I reckon I should give you a good whippin', but I'm so glad you're safe, and your ma'll be so happy to see you, I figure a good tongue-lashin' will do. Did those Indians hurt you?"

"No, pa, they didn't. But I was sure scared."

"Of course you were," Hennessey said. "You had every right to be." He looked at Captain Quincy, who had ridden up to them.

"Captain, I can't thank you enough," he said. "Every one of you Rangers."

"It's all part of the job," Quincy answered, grinning. "Now, I'd better take stock of our losses."

Aside from Shad's shoulder wound, none of the other Rangers, nor any of the Circle Dot E men, had suffered any injuries. Two or three Comanches had survived. After seeing their chief go down, they abandoned the fight, and swam their horses into Mexico. Since they were no longer a threat, the Rangers let them go. It was doubtful they'd ever return to Texas.

"Everyone's accounted for except Nate and Hoot, Dave," Bob reported. "I've got Hoot's horse here, but I figure the river took him. Nate and his horse, too. Last anyone saw of 'em they were bein' carried around that bend. Tom says Hoot got shot off his horse, and Nate apparently tried to save him, but it looks like they both drowned."

"Take a couple of the men and look for 'em, just in case," Quincy said. "We'll rest a spell, then round up the horses and head on back."

"I don't think you'll have to look for either one of 'em," Jeb said. "Here they come now."

He pointed downstream, where Nate and Hoot, riding double on an exhausted, head-hung-low Big Red, were just coming into view. Five minutes later, they reached the rest of the men.

"Boy howdy, we figured you two were goners for certain," Jeb exclaimed. "I'm sure glad to see we were wrong."

"I would've been, if it hadn't been for ol' Nate, here, savin' my bacon," Hoot said. "Thanks, pard."

"Don't mention it," Nate answered. "That's what pardners are for, to stand with each other, no matter what. You'd've done the same for me."

"Hoot, you'd better let me get that arrow out of your chest, and patch you up until we get back to the ranch, where I can treat you proper," Jim said. "I've gotta take care of Shad, too."

"I need to talk with Nate, first," Hoot said.

"That can wait. The arrow can't," Jim retorted.

"Jim, before you get to work, there's one thing I've got to say to Nate," Jeb said.

"All right, but make it quick."

"Nate, when you first came on with the Rangers, and I told you that you were a man to ride the river with, you didn't have to take me literally, son," Jeb said, laughing.

"Jeb, you just got yourself the job of buryin' those dead Indians," Quincy said. "Get outta here."

◆●◆

The arrow was removed from Hoot's chest, the wound plugged and bandaged. He was sitting against a rock, with a bandage on his chest and his left arm in a sling, smoking a cigarette. He'd asked Jim to send Nate over while the horses were gathered and the men rested, before beginning the trip back to the Circle Dot E. He waited anxiously until Nate walked up.

"How you doin', Hoot?" Nate asked. "Sorry it took me a while to get here, but I had to tend to Red."

"Aside from an arrow hole in my chest, and bein' half-drowned, I feel just fine," Hoot answered. "And you'd better have tended to Red. He saved both our lives."

"I'm glad you're gonna be okay. Hoot—"

"Nate, don't say anythin', until I say what *I* have to say," he said. "I'm obliged for what you just did, pullin' me out of that river, especially after the way I treated you. I was wrong, and I'm sorry."

"You were just mad, Hoot. Reckon I would've been too, if I'd found Consuela hangin' on you. I just wish you'd given me the chance to explain, rather'n flyin' off the handle like you did."

"I was still wrong. I know that now. I should have told you sooner, but I was too ashamed to admit it. That, and I was afraid you wouldn't believe my apology, so we could be pardners again. Just before we rode out, I asked Clarissa if she'd wait for me. Told her I'd like to get married in a year or so. You know what she did? She laughed at me. Said I wasn't good enough for her, me bein' a fiddle-footed Ranger, who'd never amount to nothin'. She also told me it was her who went after you, not the other way around, almost as if she was throwin' it in my face. Also told me she'd been with Kyle, and Ray, and two or three other cowboys. She sure made a fool outta me. I'm swearin' off women, for good. I mean it."

"Until the next pretty one comes along, and turns your

head," Nate said, smiling.

"Yeah, I guess you're right," Hood conceded. "But I sure ain't gonna get into a fight with my best friend over a gal, ever again. You can bet your hat on that, Nate. Pardners again?"

"Pardners again," Nate said. "Pardners to stand with, no matter what."

"No matter what," Hoot echoed.

◆●◆

By sundown, the Rangers and Circle Dot E men were back at the ranch. Josiah was reunited with his mother, brother, and sisters, and given the sad news of his brother Brian's death, at the hands of Black Dog. Also awaiting Captain Quincy were Ken Demarest and Phil Knight. They had returned from Presidio, with orders from Austin. Once the horses were cared for, Quincy gathered all the men in the Rangers' bunkhouse.

"Men," he said, "Our time here in the Big Bend is over. We're ridin' for San Antonio, the day after tomorrow. There's some tall trouble in the Hill Country, and we're gonna handle it. We'll take tomorrow to pack up our gear, and make a place in one of the wagons for Hoot and Diego. It'll be a while before they're able to ride. I want to thank all of you for the fine job you did on this assignment. I know you'll do just as well on our next one. That's all. Get some supper, get some rest, and be ready to pack up tomorrow."

His news was met with a chorus of cheers.

◆●◆

That night, Nate wandered up to the main house. He found Consuela on the front porch, waiting for him.

"*Hola,* Nate," she said. "You don't have to tell me. You're leaving in two days. *Senora* Hennessey already informed me. Come, sit with me for awhile."

Nate sat alongside her. He fondled the scarf she'd given him, just that morning. It still hung around his neck.

"Your scarf did bring me luck," he said. "I came back to you, like I promised. Of course, I didn't know I'd be leavin' you so soon."

"We both knew it would have to end, sometime," Consuela answered.

"It doesn't have to," Nate said. "I could ask Mr. Hennessey for a job, wranglin' horses. Then I could stay here, with you. Jeb said if I ever quit the Rangers I'd be good at workin' with horses."

"Is that what you really want, Nate, to stay here, in one place?" Consuela said. "Would that make you happy? No, *mi corazon,* I can see it in your eyes, it would not. You are not ready to settle down. Perhaps, someday, when you are, you will return, and perhaps I will still be waiting for you. But, just like you, I also am not ready to settle down. Once I have saved enough money, I shall be leaving for Santa Fe. I have cousins there, who have asked me to come live with them. So, you see, what we had was for here and now, and no more. And we still have two more evenings."

"We do, don't we?"

Nate took her in his arms, and kissed her tenderly.

About the Author

Jim Griffin became enamored of the Texas Rangers from watching the TV series, Tales of the Texas Rangers, as a youngster. He grew to be an avid student and collector of Rangers' artifacts, memorabilia and other items. His collection is now housed in the Texas Ranger Hall of Fame and Museum in Waco.

His quest for authenticity in his writing has taken him to the famous Old West towns of, Pecos, Deadwood, Cheyenne, Tombstone and numerous others. While Jim's books are fiction, he strives to keep them as accurate as possible within the realm of fiction.

A graduate of Southern Connecticut State University, Jim now divides his time between Branford, Connecticut and Keene, New Hampshire when he isn't travelling around the west.

A devoted and enthusiastic horseman, Jim bought his first horse when he was a junior in college. He has owned several American Paint horses. He is a member of the Connecticut Horse Council Volunteer Horse Patrol, an organization which assists the state park Rangers with patrolling parks and forests.

Jim's books are traditional Westerns in the best sense of the term, portraying strong heroes with good character and moral values. Highly reminiscent of the pulp westerns of yesteryear, the heroes and villains are clearly separated.

Jim was initially inspired to write at the urging of

friend and author James Reasoner. After the successful publication of his first book, Trouble Rides the Texas Pacific, published in 2005, Jim was encouraged to continue his writing.

Website: www.jamesjgriffin.net

Coming Soon: Lone Star Ranger 6: A Ranger Gone Bad

A RANGER TO RIDE WITH by James J. Griffin

Book 1

Nathaniel Stewart's life changes in the blink of an eye when his family is murdered by a band of marauding raiders. They've made one terrible mistake...they didn't finish the job. Fourteen-year-old Nathaniel is very much alive and ready to exact the justice his mother, father, and older brother deserve. Taken in by a company of Texas Rangers, he begins to learn what it means to survive in the rugged wilds of Texas.

A RANGER TO RECKON WITH by James J. Griffin

Book 2

As the youngest man in the company of Texas Rangers he's riding with, Nate Stewart discovers he's got a lot to learn. Determined to find the brutal gang of raiders who murdered his family and left him for dead on the Texas plains, Nate must grow up fast. When he comes face-to-face with the pale-eyed devil responsible for the deaths of his parents and older brother, will Nate be able to finally get his revenge?

A RANGER TO FIGHT WITH by James J. Griffin

Book 3

When Captain Quincy's company of Rangers is ordered to the Big Bend, Nate has no choice but to ride with them. It appears his odds of finding the men who murdered his family grow more distant with each passing mile. Will Nate and his Ranger companions finally catch up with the killers? Nate's gut feeling says they will—but who will survive?

A RANGER'S CHRISTMAS by James J. Griffin

Book 4

Nate Stewart has avenged the deaths of his family by seeing their pale-eyed murderer dead. But his days of being a Texas Ranger have only just begun. With Christmas on the way, and the Rangers sent to the Big Bend area to patrol, they're faced with everything from a buffalo stampede to having to resort to finding water any way they can even if it means taking it by force. When Nate believes he may have accidentally killed a friend, he falls into danger that leaves the Rangers believing he's been drowned. Can a Christmas miracle save him and reunite him with Captain Quincy's men for A RANGER'S CHRISTMAS?

Made in the USA
Middletown, DE
08 April 2015